"Help!"

As Jemma lunged, the ladder slipped sideways, and she clung to the shelving while the metal contraption crashed to the floor.

A shriek tore from Jemma's throat. With her heart racing, she inched her feet more firmly onto the new display units. From somewhere behind her, a bang and thudding footsteps sounded. "Hurry, Claire. I'm petrified," she called to her mother-in-law.

The metal clanged below. Then the ladder appeared alongside her. Jemma moved her foot to the nearest rung. Feeling safer, she secured her hands and feet to the metal and hands braced her from behind.

"Thank you, Claire," Jemma sang.

"You're welcome," an amused baritone voice rumbled.

Jemma tensed and pivoted her head, gazing down into a pair of electric blue eyes canopied by a thatch of salt-and-pepper hair.

Books by Gail Gaymer Martin

Love Inspired

Upon a Midnight Clear #117
Secrets of the Heart #147
A Love for Safekeeping #161
Loving Treasures #177

GAIL GAYMER MARTIN

lives with her real-life hero in Lathrup Village, Michigan. Growing up in nearby Madison Heights, Gail wrote poems and stories as a child and progressed to professional journals, skits and poems for teachers, and programs for her church. When she retired she tried her hand at her dream—writing novels.

Gail is multipublished in nonfiction and fiction with ten novels and five novellas, and many more to come. Her Steeple Hill Love Inspired romance *Upon a Midnight Clear* won a Holt Medallion in 2001. Besides writing, Gail enjoys singing, public speaking and presenting writers' workshops. She believes that God's gift of humor gets her through even the darkest moment and praises God for His blessings.

She loves to hear from her readers. Write to her on the Internet at martinga@aol.com or at P.O. Box 760063, Lathrup Village, MI 48076.

Loving Treasures
Gail Gaymer Martin

Love Inspired®

Published by Steeple Hill Books™

STEEPLE HILL BOOKS

Steeple
Hill™

ISBN 0-373-87184-8

LOVING TREASURES

Don't urge me to leave you or to turn back
from you. Where you go I will go,
and where you stay I will stay. Your people
will be my people and your God my God.

—*Ruth* 1:16

To my stepfather, Clayton Riley,
who is one of my biggest and proudest fans

Thanks to Walter A. Lucken III
for his sailing expertise,
and in memory of Rite (Mémé) who inspired Claire

Chapter One

"What was that?"

Jemma Dupre paused amid the merchandise cartons being readied for display and cocked her ear toward the odd whine coming from the half-filled shelves.

Moving around a pile of boxes, she heard the sound again—a cat's plaintive "meow." *Bodkin.* Shaking her head, Jemma followed the mournful grumble to the wall adjacent to the boutique's front display window.

As she gazed high above her head at one of the new stock racks, Bodkin paced along the top shelf with proud indignation like a spread-tailed peacock, his own gray-striped tail flicking with annoyance.

"You silly cat. You got yourself up there. Get yourself down," Jemma said, hands on her hips.

Unmindful, Bodkin only stared at her and released another pitiful cry.

Jemma called over her shoulder, "Claire, your goofy cat is in trouble." She listened for her mother-in-law's response. Nothing. "Claire?"

Hearing no response, Jemma stepped toward the back of the boutique, then paused remembering her mother-in-law had said something about running to the hardware store. To Jemma's consternation, Claire seemed determined to single-handedly organize the new boutique in a day...that is, with Jemma's assistance.

But Jemma was little help. She was too short, too thin and too helpless. On top of that, her mind had clogged with the changes she'd faced the past few months. Because Claire, her deceased husband's mother, was the only family she had, she'd left her small home in Monroe, Michigan, and moved to the village of Loving. Now she wondered if she'd made the right decision.

Bodkin grumbled again. Irritated by the cat's nagging, Jemma returned to her rescue mission. Scanning the room, she spied the painter's ladder lying nearby on the floor. She edged it against the wall, then stepped back and peered at the contraption and hesitated. Height and Jemma were not best friends.

As she eyed the metal structure, Jemma's legs trembled at the thought of climbing the thing to chase after Bodkin. If not for the cat's incessant complaining, Jemma would have waited for Claire to return. But it was more than she could bear.

"How did you get up there?" she asked the cat, who hung over the shelf edge, staring down at her with squinted, chartreuse eyes.

She shifted the ladder close to the cat's perch and peered up at Bodkin. "If you don't come down, I'll have to climb up there to get you." Her fists clenched at her sides. "So please come down," she pleaded. The tabby peered at her without the flick of a whisker.

Finally, with rising trepidation, Jemma placed her right foot on the first rung, then lifted her left. Faltering, she climbed one step, paused, then took another, praying the cat would stay within her reach.

No such blessing. With the floor six rungs below her, Jemma extended her arms, coaxing the retreating tabby. But Bodkin continued backing away.

Jemma studied the situation. If she shifted the ladder closer, she'd have to climb down, then up again. And Bodkin would probably skitter farther away.

Frustrated, she drew in a breath and propped her left foot on the new shelving, then stretched her arms, hoping to grab the nervous cat. As she lunged, the ladder slipped sideways, and Jemma clung to the shelving while the metal contraption crashed to the floor.

A shriek tore from Jemma's throat. With her heart racing, she inched her feet more firmly onto the new display units while desperately hanging onto the top shelf. Bodkin rested beside Jemma's white-knuckled grasp and licked her fingers with a raspy pink tongue.

"You dumb cat," she breathed. "Claire!" she screamed, in a futile hope that her mother-in-law had returned. Only silence and her fearful gasps filled the air. In desperation, she opened her mouth and bellowed, "Help!"

From somewhere behind her, a bang and thudding footsteps sounded. Her arms quivered with tension and her chest heaved as she struggled for air from lungs frozen with panic. The strides drew nearer.

"Hurry, Claire! The ladder slipped. I'm petrified."

The metal clanged below. Then the ladder appeared alongside her. Jemma moved one foot to the nearest rung and felt Claire's hurried movement climbing the ladder. Feeling safer, she secured her hands and feet to the metal, as Claire's hands braced her from behind.

"Thank you. Thank you." Jemma sang it like a litany.

"You're welcome," an amused baritone voice rumbled at her back.

Jemma tensed and pivoted her head, gazing down into a pair of electric-blue eyes canopied by a thatch of salt-and-pepper hair.

"Who are you?" she asked as fear shot through her. In a death grip, she clung to the rung with one hand and pushed against his shoulder with the other, realizing that the stranger's hands were wrapped around her waist.

Laughter rippled from this throat as he backed down, his eyes riveted to hers. "I might ask you the same question," he said. "But I'd guess you're Claire's new clerk."

Claire's new clerk. The pathetic words charged through her, and pride ruffled her gratitude. "I'm the owner's daughter-in-law," she said, peering at him.

"Ah," he said, stepping back from the ladder as she descended, "then, you must be Lyle's wife." His face twisted in an undefined expression.

Jemma's foot touched the security of the floor and she unclamped her aching hand from the rung. "I was. Lyle died a year ago. I'm Jemma Dupre."

His face washed with muddied emotion. "Ah yes, Claire told me. I'm very sorry."

Puzzled by the stranger, Jemma swallowed her mixed emotions. "Thank you."

A serious expression had replaced his amusement. "So, you're Jemma." Towering above her five foot two inches, impressive in an obviously expensive sport coat, he thrust his hand toward her. "I'm Philip Somerville. Claire's cousin."

"Philip Somerville." Dismayed at her brusqueness, she covered her mouth with her hand. "I'm so sorry. I hope I wasn't rude. Claire didn't mention you were coming today."

"That's because I didn't tell her." He glanced over his shoulder. "Where is she, by the way?"

"The hardware for—"

Bodkin's plaintive cry halted her in mid-sentence.

"Oh-oh, I forgot about you, Mr. Bodkin." She gazed up at the tabby and rubbed the back of her neck. "He'll have to wait until Claire comes back."

"Let me," Philip said, grasping the ladder and moving up the rungs with the confidence of a fireman. "Come here, my furry friend," he said, nabbing the cat by the collar and nestling it against his chest.

When he placed the tabby on the floor, Bodkin arched his back, aimed an evil "hiss" at Philip, then strode off as if he'd been offended.

"He has an attitude," Jemma said, apologizing for the cat's ungrateful behavior.

Philip smiled. "No problem. I've learned to take customers' complaints in stride."

Jemma pulled data from her memory bank. "Right," she said, pleased that she remembered. "You own a resort on Lake Michigan."

"Guilty," he said, sending her a humble grin. Turning in a full circle, he peered around the room. "I hope Claire is pleased with the shop. I made the best deal for her that I could."

"Oh, she's thrilled, and with the apartment upstairs, it's perfect."

"It's rather small, but I figured it would do for now. When you two find something larger and more permanent, you can rent out the space overhead."

When you two find something larger. Jemma's mind bogged. She had no plans to stay forever with Claire. She'd depended on her mother-in-law too much already. As soon as she got herself together and helped Claire set up the shop, she'd find her own place...and a job. "It'll do fine." She pushed her thoughts aside, not willing to share them.

"Whatever you decide," he said, amusement swimming in his eyes.

Jemma clutched at the neck of her T-shirt. His distracting grin and blue eyes sent uncomfortable jitters up her back.

"You'll work here, I hope," he said, filling in the silence.

She tried to come up with something evasive, but nothing came to mind. She had to be honest. "Only to help Claire open the shop."

He tilted his head with a quizzical look.

"I doubt if a new boutique will support two women," Jemma continued. "I'll need to find my own job once things are settled."

His pensive face brightened. "Let me know when you're ready to make a move. I'm sure I can find a spot for you at the resort."

Jemma faltered. She'd had enough charity to last her a lifetime, but she couldn't explain that to a virtual stranger. "Thanks." She dismissed his offer. "I'm—"

"Philip!"

Claire's vibrant deep voice hit her ears, and Jemma pivoted in her mother-in-law's direction.

The older woman bounded across the room, looking impulsive and exotic in her ankle-length Indian-print dress and her long, auburn, windblown hair.

"Claire," Philip said, taking her in his arms with a warm hug. "You look well." His gaze traveled the length of her solid, large-boned frame. "In fact, unbelievable."

"Thank you, Philip. It's so good to see you finally. I'd hoped you'd stop by." She beckoned him to follow. "Come into the back."

Jemma peered at Philip as he strode alongside Claire, wondering if his "unbelievable" was a cover for his shock at Claire's outlandish getup.

When she'd first met her mother-in-law, Jemma had blinked in amazement at the older woman's reddish, flyaway hair and her eccentric costume—zebra-striped spandex pants with a black gauze peasant blouse. But Jemma soon learned that Claire's heart was as lavish and generous as her flamboyant clothing. The elderly woman was giving, good-natured, and easy to love.

Waiting until they passed through the workroom doorway, Jemma gathered her thoughts before following. When she joined them in the back room, Philip was seated at the large worktable, while Claire stood with her back to them beside the microwave, heating water.

"Sorry it's taken me so long to come by," Philip said.

"Don't fret. I appreciate everything you did for me, Philip, but I wanted to thank you in person. The shop's perfect." She spun around, dangling a tea bag from her fingers. "I know it wasn't easy with my meager savings, and—"

"To be honest, Claire," Philip said, "speaking of your savings, I had to add a little backing to yours to make this deal come about. But please don't worry, I know I'll get it back."

Claire's face sagged, and she lowered her head for a moment before lifting her misted eyes. "That was too kind, Philip. You've already done so much for me."

He raised his hand to quiet her. "Don't say a word. Please. Sharing my good fortune with family is no problem." A distant longing flashed in his eyes before he turned to Jemma. "In fact, I've offered…"

Jemma's inner voice cried "no" as she struggled to keep the grimace from distorting her expression.

Apparently noting her panic, Philip's words trailed off. "I'm really glad that you came back home, Claire."

Grateful that he had altered his comment, Jemma unknotted her fingers. She was sure Philip had been about to refer to his job offer, and she had yet to tell Claire that she planned to strike out on her own as soon as things were settled.

The microwave sounded. Claire opened the door and plunged a tea bag into the mug of hot water, gave it to Philip, then made another and handed it to Jemma.

With the steaming cup clutched in her hand,

Jemma slid into a seat at the table, listening to Claire's vision of the shop and her hope for success.

Jemma prayed for her mother-in-law's well-being. Life had not been easy for Claire, either. Like father, like son. Both men had squandered money and left their widows close to penniless except for a small insurance policy. Claire had sold her home for the bulk of her investment money. Without Philip's kindness, what would they have done?

Filled with questions, Jemma studied the handsome, graying man. Was he another type-A personality that lived for his work with no time for God? Between her father-in-law and Lyle, she'd had her fill of men like that. She had one conciliatory thought. Philip had not squandered his money. He seemed to be a wealthy man.

Jemma brought her mind back to the present, as Claire slid a bag of rock-hard sugar cookies on the table, then whirled back toward the microwave to extract her mug. Instead of joining them at the table, she leaned against the counter.

"The sign painters are coming tomorrow. I've named the shop Loving Treasures. What do you think?"

Though she directed the question to Philip, Jemma answered. "I like it." Jemma had tossed the name around in her thoughts for the past couple of days and decided Loving Treasures had a ring to it. Focusing on Philip, she waited for his response.

Instead his silent gaze shifted from one to the other.

Seeming undisturbed by his silence, Claire swept toward them and plopped into a chair. "So much to do. I'd like to open next week." She grabbed a sugar cookie from the package and clamped it between her teeth, but with a grunt and scowl she plucked it from her mouth and dropped it to the table. "I need to find a dentist," she said, rubbing the upper gum line. "I have a sore spot. Dentures, you know."

To Jemma's discomfort, Claire put her hand up to her mouth as if to remove them, then thought better, and halted.

"Back in a minute," Claire said, hurrying from the room.

Jemma shifted her uneasy gaze toward Phillip, but his focus was on the doorway.

In a moment, Claire returned, patting the pocket of her exotic print dress. "There," she said, "I feel better already."

Amusement flickered across Philip's lips before his expression faded to a concerned scowl. "You need to take care of those teeth. Boyd Barrow's office is right up the street about a block. He's a good dentist and a friend. Give him a call."

"Barrow, huh?" Claire repeated. "Thanks, suppose I should." She recaptured the abandoned cookie, gnawed at it with her gums, and chattered on about the shop while flashing him an occasional toothless grin as if she had a million-dollar smile.

Mortified, Jemma stared off in space. She'd heard the plans many times, so her thoughts drifted easily to Philip. With curiosity, she tried to guess his age. His graying hair contradicted his youthful demeanor. Only a splay of crow's feet at the corner of his striking eyes added a dash of seasoned charm to his good looks.

He wore his hair trim, yet long enough to comb back into a full sweep of waves. A hint of five-o'clock shadow outlined Philip's jaw and drew her focus to his full pleasant mouth. His easy smile warmed her. Generous and kind is how she imagined him—and thoughtful.

Occasionally Philip's gaze drifted to Jemma. His look made her uncomfortable. She wondered if she had crumbs on her cheek, or maybe he was just sizing her up for his job offer. If he could read her mind, he'd know she'd do anything rather than accept any more humbling kindness from anyone. She needed to build confidence by taking care of herself.

Philip rose, drawing her back to the conversation. "It looks like you have things under control," he said, sliding the chair into place. "But don't do too much, Claire, even if it takes two weeks before you open. And if you need anything at all…" His gaze drifted to Jemma. "Either of you, please let me know."

A pinwheel whirled in Jemma's chest, taking her breath away. No one had ever given her that much kind attention, not even Lyle. She murmured her thanks and sat nailed to her seat, while Claire followed him to the side door. His rich, genial voice drifted from the hallway.

Drawn to follow, Jemma rose and hovered behind them. Before he disappeared through the door, Philip gave her a summer-breeze smile, sending her internal pinwheel on another merry spin.

Philip pulled open his car door and slid inside, his attention locked to the large boutique window. The petite outline of the charming young woman he'd just met shimmered behind the pane and through him like a flutter of fine silk. He closed the car door, turned the key and rolled down the window to enjoy the warm spring air. He wished he could recapture the alluring scent that had filled him when he rescued Jemma from the ladder. Leaning back in his seat, he focused through the windshield on Jemma in the shop's interior.

Yet, much more than glass and space separated them. While he watched her, Jemma leaned into the large display window and adjusted the drape of a black shawl around a faceless, gold-painted mannequin's shoulders. When Jemma straightened her back, her trim, delicate figure looked fragile like spring grass...fresh and new. Lovely.

He shook his head. "You old geezer," he muttered aloud, "she's probably two decades younger than you. You ought to be ashamed." Still, she'd rustled feelings in him that he hadn't felt in years—

even before Susan died. He wondered if she had enjoyed his hands around her waist as much as he had.

Shifting into reverse, he eased the luxury car around then rolled into a break in traffic. He was forty-nine. Fifty in a few weeks. Jemma was at the most thirty, he speculated. A child compared to him.

He faltered. Was it attraction or pity he felt? Lyle rose in his mind. Lyle the wastrel, Claire's good-for-nothing son. How had he captured a beauty like Jemma? She seemed like a true gentlewoman.

Philip thought back to Lyle's glib tongue—a way with words Philip had always wished for himself—and answered his own question. Lyle had been handsome and charming. Not until someone knew him well would they see the unpleasant side, the squandering playboy beneath the boyish smile. Lyle was like his father.

Naive, trusting Jemma probably fell for his beguiling ways. And what did she have to show for her marriage? He was certain she had nothing.

Nothing. The thought struck him. What did he have? Material things, yes. But no family. A wife who died far too young. A brother who'd walked away from the family. Who was he to judge Jemma's life?

When he spotted Boyd's office building, Philip pulled into the strip parking area and turned off the motor. To help his cousin's finances, Philip had decided to have Boyd put Claire's bill on his account.

He strode toward the entrance, hitting the remote

to lock the car. Philip passed the list of doctors' names and room numbers, turned left and headed down the corridor. Dr. Boyd Barrow, DDS appeared on the brass doorplate. Inside, a lone patient flipped through a magazine.

Philip stepped to the small counter, but before he spoke, the clerk acknowledged him by name. "The doctor should be free in a minute, Mr. Somerville."

He gestured toward the waiting gentleman.

"He's waiting for the hygienist," she whispered.

Philip sank into the armless, vinyl chair and eyed the wall decor—plaster images of teeth before and after braces, posters of various stages of gum decay, and two seemingly out-of-place seascape prints.

His first thoughts drifted to Claire's toothless grin, but in a heartbeat, Jemma's fragile face and generous smile filled his thoughts. Why was he tormenting himself? She was only a girl...no, she was a woman. Jemma was a lovely, young woman who deserved an equally handsome, virile and fit young man. She wouldn't want some gray-haired coot.

Anyway, he'd messed up one woman's life. He was a bad husband. Why would he allow even fleeting thoughts of Jemma to puncture his world? She deserved better.

"You can see the doctor now, Mr. Somerville."

Philip's gaze shot up to the young woman in the doorway. She strode away, returning to the computer and telephone. He rose and followed the well-known path to Boyd's office. He'd been a miserable husband, but maybe being a generous cousin would help atone for his past neglect. Maybe, God would know he was sorry. More than sorry, he was penitent.

Chapter Two

Jemma massaged the tension in her neck and leaned back against Claire's sofa. She'd brought none of her own furniture with her. Most of it had been frayed and worn anyway. Today, she'd made her decision and knew that she had to talk with her mother-in-law. Independence was what Jemma needed.

Though she was grateful to Claire, living with her for any length of time could only damage their loving relationship. Her mother-in-law had a surplus of eccentricity in dress and behavior, but her head for business was Jemma's major concern. Could Claire manage the shop without giving away the merchandise?

Jemma cringed, recalling a day shortly after she'd met her mother-in-law when she'd expressed admiration for one of Claire's silk scarves. The woman had yanked it from her neck and flung it across

Jemma's shoulders, insisting it was a gift. Nothing would change her mind. After another such display of generosity, Jemma had been afraid to compliment any accessory or clothing of her mother-in-law's. A guest could easily find himself leaving Claire's, carrying her sofa.

Taking a sip of herbal tea, Jemma savored the soothing, subtle flavor. She swiveled her head from side to side to release the tension. Her gaze drifted around the cozy apartment—better for one than two—wondering what the future held for her.

With the coming of summer and tourists, the local newspaper offered a list of sales positions, the only work experience she had, but all those that Jemma had phoned started at minimum wage. If she didn't earn a larger salary, she'd be forced to stay in the apartment.

Although she guessed Claire would be satisfied with that, Claire wasn't the problem. It was Jemma. She had felt beholden far too long. Now that the shop was open, she needed to make her way in the world—stretch her wings and fly. She yearned to carve her own niche in Loving.

Loving. The word triggered two intermingled thoughts: the friendly village where the postman already greeted her by name…and Philip's warm smile.

Thinking of him, disappointment fluttered down Jemma's spine. She hadn't seen Philip since the day he saved her from the fallen ladder. He'd called once to see how Claire was doing, but not since. Each time the bell chimed on the boutique door, Jemma looked up nervously, hoping to see him saunter into the shop with his bright grin.

She blocked the thought. Foolish dreams. Philip had a business—make that many businesses—to run. He had no time for an impoverished, secondhand relative. He was kind enough to take on Claire, but he owed Jemma nothing.

She rose, rinsed the teacup, and placed it in the sink. Time she returned to the shop. Business often picked up in the late morning, especially on cloudy days when the spring tourists were less likely to head to the beach or to the pier for lake excursions. Drawing a deep breath, Jemma charged down the stairs to the boutique.

At the counter, Claire appeared to have two elderly women spellbound. No one could gussy up a story or her attire like her mother-in-law, and today was no exception. She was draped in a red-and-gold Japanese print caftan with a large Fuji mum pinned in her wild, upswept hair.

Claire turned Jemma's way and flagged her over. "Come meet Abby and Silva Hartmann. They own that pretty bed and breakfast farther down Washington."

Jemma extended her hand as she approached. "The Loving Arms?" she asked.

The taller woman responded. "Yes, don't you love

the name. We thought of Jesus welcoming the little children.'' She took Jemma's hand. "I'm Abby.''

"How do you do?'' Jemma said, trying not to smile at the woman's exuberance.

"Silva here,'' the other one said, jutting her fingers forward. "Or call me Sissy. I answer to both.''

Jemma smiled and squeezed her hand. "Nice to meet you, Silva.''

The woman inched close to Jemma's ear. "We're really a boarding house, dear, but Abby thought 'bed and breakfast' sounded more charming. Don't you agree?''

Jemma nodded, her curiosity growing, but another customer wandered into the shop and caught her attention.

She made a polite retreat, as Claire drew them back with her sales pitch. "Now about this lovely handbag. I have an elegant scarf that picks up this rich burgundy shade.''

Jemma stifled a grin and headed toward the other customer, her mind tangled in the rooming-house news. She'd check later, in private, to ask the Hartmanns about their rates.

The customer was "just looking," so Jemma gave her space and shifted to a disheveled display of leather goods: wallets, coin purses, picture holders. As she organized the items, a warm hand touched her arm.

She turned, expecting Claire or the customer, but instead, her heart did a flip-flop when she saw the hand's owner. "Philip." She prayed her face hadn't flushed. "How are you?"

"Fine, and you?" he asked.

Her answer tripped over her tongue. She felt foolish, like a preteen experiencing her first amorous attraction.

"You look well," he said, filling the silence.

She swallowed her embarrassment. "Oh, ah, I'm just...I'm okay. Fine." She reined her uncontrolled thoughts. "Yes, I'm fine."

His lopsided grin faded as he pivoted his head, viewing the completed displays. "Very nice. And Claire has some business, too, I see."

Jemma found her voice. "Well, some. It's growing each day."

"When the summer tourists arrive, she'll do fine. This is a good location." He turned from Claire. "So what are your plans? You've decided to stay here with Claire?"

Jemma squirmed under his gaze. "No," she said, lowering her voice, "but I haven't talked with her yet. I'm hoping she won't be disappointed. I've been looking for a job, mainly in the newspaper, but haven't really found—"

He touched her arm. "Did you forget my offer?"

Unable to look at him without feeling addled, Jemma lowered her head. "No, but I thought I'd look around on my own."

His hand dropped to his side. "The resort's large,

Jemma. You'll have to see the place. In summer, we're busy. It's crazy.''

Not knowing what he wanted her to say, she didn't respond.

He caught her chin and tilted it upward. ''I hire new people all the time, Jemma. I'm not offering you a handout.''

''I know,'' she said, wishing he'd let her collect her thoughts.

As if reading her mind, he lowered his fingers, gave her arm a squeeze and dropped his hand without further comment.

When he turned toward Claire, Jemma breathed a relieved sigh. She followed Philip's lead, watching Claire ring up the Hartmann sisters' sale. The package was small, so Jemma concluded it wasn't the handbag but the scarf. Abby and Silva left the shop, with their small purchase.

Claire closed the register, then noticed her company. ''Philip,'' she said, coming from behind the counter. ''You've been a stranger.''

''I know. I was out of town on business for a few days.'' He gave the shop an admiring once-over. ''The store looks great.''

''It's not a madhouse, but we're doing okay, and I'm keeping an ear open to the customers' wants.''

''Good. Always tune in to the trends.''

''Within reason,'' Jemma added, wondering if Philip really knew Claire all that well.

He eyed her, arching a brow. "Well, sure, within reason. I'd steer clear of elephants." He chuckled.

Though Jemma laughed, she feared she saw a sparkle of interest in Claire's eyes.

Philip tucked his hand into his pants pocket. "Now, let's get down to business."

Claire's eyes widened.

"My birthday is Saturday, and I wondered if you ladies would join me for dinner. I thought you might like to see the resort before the summer crowd."

"We'd love it," Claire said. "I've been wanting to drop by."

Without comment, Philip shifted his focus to Jemma and waited.

Discomfort flooded through her, and when she spoke, her voice sounded muffled in her ears. "That would be nice." For a moment, she wondered if she'd really spoken the words.

"Great," Philip said. "What time does the shop close Saturday?"

"Seven," Claire answered. "We'll be ready."

Jemma tuned out the final conversation, struggling with her ridiculous emotions. She'd been a widow for nearly two years and hadn't felt a smidgeon of longing for male companionship. So why now was her pulse tripping through her veins like that of a toddler enjoying her first spring day?

Trying to look interested, Jemma nodded and smiled. She heard herself say goodbye as Philip headed toward the door, but her inner voice was louder, warning her to beware. All she would find was more heartache.

A hand pressed against Philip's shoulder, and he drew back in irritation. This was the third interruption during his birthday dinner. When the first had occurred, he realized he should have invited Jemma and Claire to the Inn at Spring Lake. Though they wouldn't have seen the resort, they would have had privacy and solitude there.

"Can't it wait?" he asked, trying to give the high sign to Ian, his executive assistant whom he'd coerced to work nights.

"It's your brother."

The filet Philip had eaten minutes earlier churned in his stomach. He hadn't heard from Andrew in a couple of years. "My brother?" He rose. "You're sure?"

Ian Barry nodded, fingered the frame of his eyeglasses and stepped back.

"I'm sorry," Philip said to the women, excusing himself and following Ian between the tables toward the office telephone.

Why was Andrew calling him after all this time? Resentment reared its head. Even their father's funeral had done no more than motivate a floral bouquet and a briefly scrawled note of apology for not returning home. Philip swallowed the bile that rose to his throat. Civility—that's all he could muster.

Inside the office he grasped the telephone, his

clammy palm cooling to icy fingers. Before he dismissed his assistant, Ian stepped out of the room and closed the door.

"Andrew," Philip said, struggling to keep his voice controlled.

He listened to his brother's hesitant voice, apologizing for his detachment from the family.

Philip waited for the plea he anticipated. He was sure Andrew had run out of money, that he needed a little help until his "ship came in," that he expected a windfall on Monday. He waited, but no plea came.

"Why are you calling, Andrew?" Philip asked. He heard his voice take on an edge. "It's been over two years since we talked."

"I know," Andrew said, "and I'm sorry. I've had a lot of time to think, Philip, and…ah, I wanted to wish you a happy birthday."

Philip stared at the receiver unable to speak. *Happy birthday?* No. There had to be more.

"Are you there, Philip?"

Andrew's voice tugged him from his confused thoughts. "Yes, I'm here. You mean…that's it? You called to wish me a happy birthday?"

This time Andrew was silent.

"I'm sorry," Philip said. "What I said was uncalled for. Thanks. I'm pleased you remembered."

"I do remember."

Struggling to grasp the call, Philip pictured Jemma and Claire waiting for him to return. "It's good to hear from you, Andrew, but I really should get back to my guests. Cousin Claire is waiting for me…and Lyle's wife…er, widow, Jemma. Lyle died a while ago.''

As they spoke their goodbyes, Andrew's voice faded and left Philip feeling sadly empty. After he replaced the receiver, he stood a moment, calming his emotions and rousing his spirit. Today was his birthday—his fiftieth. That, in itself, was depressing enough.

Jemma's lovely face drifted through his mind. So many years had passed since a woman had yanked on the strings of his heart. But Jemma did. He had no idea why. He pondered the reason as he hurried back to the table.

Seeing Jemma from a distance, his heartstrings received a firm tug. She looked lovely in a pale green sheath with a simple strand of pearls. Like dew on a summer morning: soft, delicate and intangible. Jemma was a secret place and he longed for the key to open the door to the wonderful surprises he might find there.

The thought of his fiftieth birthday struck him like a sledgehammer. To calm his thoughts, he settled his gaze on Claire.

He'd controlled a chuckle when he arrived at the apartment earlier. Claire had greeted him in a flurry of purplish chiffon that carried him back to the archives of early television: Donna Reed, Loretta Young, Lucille Ball. While Jemma was a spring flower, Claire had all the outlandish glitz of the New Orleans Mardi Gras.

"Sorry," Philip said as he slipped into his chair. "I owe you both a quiet dinner somewhere else. I should have known better."

"No problem," Claire said, waving away his apology. "So how's Andrew?"

"Fine, I think. He called to wish me a happy birthday." Philip still hadn't sifted through the phone call. It had left him curious and concerned.

"Andrew's been away a long time," Claire said.

Philip nodded. "Over four years, I think. He didn't come back for Dad's funeral."

"I know," she said. "It was a shame."

Jemma only listened to the conversation, and Philip wondered if she were bored or distracted. If he didn't do something soon to liven the celebration, they'd go home thinking the evening was a disaster.

Philip lifted his cup and sipped the unappealing lukewarm coffee. Sliding the drink onto the saucer, he placed his palms against the table edge and leaned forward. "How about a tour?"

As if they'd heard their morning alarm clock, both women's heads shot up.

"I've bored you long enough with untold interruptions. Would you like to see what we have to offer here?"

He rose and his guests followed. He could hear the click of their heels hitting the wooden floor as they reached the resort lobby.

Philip looked at the entrance with pride. A large Tabriz carpet covered the oak planks in the center of the room, creating a conversation setting of love seats and arm chairs. He'd put in many hours trying to create the perfect balance between comfort and elegance.

"Let me show you one of our guest rooms," Philip said.

They waited while he located the key of an unoccupied room. After they'd admired the massive suite and the expansive balcony overlooking Lake Michigan, he led them from the main lodge, passing the spa and indoor pool, to a small cottage beyond the shuffleboard and tennis courts. As they returned, Claire lagged behind.

Philip halted. "I'm wearing you out," he said, focusing on his cousin.

"A little," she said, sinking into a canvas chair next to an umbrella table. "But don't let me stop you." She gave a swish of her hand, her fingers weighted with two garish rings. "You young ones finish the tour. Please. I'll sit here and enjoy the sunset."

"Are you sure?" Jemma asked, her focus shifting from Claire to Philip and back. "I hate to leave you—"

"It's a gift," Claire said. "I don't often have a chance to sit in a lovely place like this. Please—" she motioned again toward the flower gardens

"—enjoy yourselves."

Philip accepted her offer and, taking Jemma's elbow, steered her toward the gardens and the path down to the water's edge.

Even in dress pumps, Jemma seemed petite beside him. A thin strap hung over her shoulder and the small purse swung at her side like a pendulum. She was quiet, and he longed to ask questions, to pry, to learn more about her. Had she been brutally unhappy with Lyle? Why hadn't she had children? Perhaps a little daughter with Jemma's gentle smile and thoughtful green eyes... Where would Jemma live when she left Claire's? And why wouldn't she accept his offer of employment?

Jemma stopped and surveyed the gardens. "This is lovely," she said. "Do you have a gardener?"

He chuckled, wondering if she thought he weeded and divided rhizomes in his free time. His smile faded, seeing her embarrassment.

"That was a dumb question. Obviously, someone takes care of all this property." She swung her hand in a wide gesture, motioning to the spacious spread of grass and landscape.

"It wasn't dumb," he said, wishing he could retract his chuckle. "I have a groundskeeper and he has a crew. Their biggest job is the golf course. No one's fussier than weekend golfers."

Though she grinned, he imagined she didn't know a thing about the game. Aware of Claire's difficult past, he could only guess that Jemma's life wasn't much better.

They followed the walkway toward the lake. In the setting sun, the summer rays danced on Jemma's golden curls. A flaxen wisp of hair had blown loose in the breeze and coiled against her cheek. Philip longed to capture the strand and bury his face in the exotic fragrance he'd inhaled on their first meeting.

Confounded by his thoughts, he pointed toward the short pier where guests could toss out a line and catch a striped bass or lake trout. The white sand stretched along the shore where, later in the summer, guests would work on a tan, read a paperback or build castles with their children.

Children. Jemma would be a perfect mother, he speculated. Again, he longed to probe, but didn't.

They walked to the end of the empty pier and stood in silence as the sun spilled its flaming hues into the watery horizon.

"Philip, this is beautiful." Jemma tilted her head and looked into his eyes.

He clamped his lips together to avoid speaking. Nothing was more beautiful than this woman. Without hesitation, he lifted his finger and pushed the curl from her cheek. Though her skin was cool, fire shot through his veins. He jerked back. "I shouldn't have done that," he said, as much to himself as in apology to Jemma.

"I can't seem to control it," she said. "Naturally curly hair has a mind of its own."

She smiled, he clenched his jaw in an attempt to control the unbidden emotions that galloped through him.

Philip turned his attention to the horizon and hummed "Happy Birthday" inside his head. He was fifty. He had to keep reminding himself.

Jemma left the boutique through the front door. She'd told Claire she had a few errands to run, but guilt filled her, knowing she was on her way to speak with the Hartmann sisters about their rooming house.

With her mind jumping from one thought to another, she headed up the street, praying that God would help her make good decisions. The first thing she needed the Lord to handle was Philip. Trying to sleep was impossible. As soon as her head hit the pillow, Philip's amused grin monopolized her mind—as did his thick thatch of graying hair, his probing eyes and his gentle manner.

Yet mingled in his kindness was a drive and industry that reminded her too much of Lyle. She knew the comparison was foolish. Lyle had lost every penny he invested. Obviously, Philip was a wealthy man. But Lyle had no time for God, and she assumed a man like Philip Somerville wouldn't have time for God, either. Nor time for marriage and a family.

Feeling a rising heat, Jemma touched her cheeks. She hated her fair skin that always signaled her discomfort. Why would she even consider marriage and family in the same moment she thought of Philip?

Her pulse mounted as she walked, and she concentrated on her vanishing good sense, praying for self-control.

She slowed, checking the house numbers. When she spotted the address, she stopped. She stood on the sidewalk in front of a solid stone house, the sprawling front porch filled with pots of flowers and a glider swing.

Attached to the railing was an oval sign announcing the Hartmann's residence, Loving Arms. Jemma grinned, remembering Sissy's explanation—Jesus welcoming the little children. That's what Jemma needed. Jesus's open, loving arms waiting to shield her from hurt and ready to give her strength.

She bounded up the porch stairs and rang the bell. With the front door open, she heard a bustle from inside. Peering through the screen, she saw Abby Hartmann rush down the stairs as Sissy rounded the corner. They reached the door together.

"Hello," Abby said, obviously the more outgoing of the two. "You're Jemma from the boutique."

"Yes, Jemma Dupre," she said, stepping back as Abby pushed open the screen.

"Come in. Please." With a flutter of arms, the woman sent Sissy on her way to make tea and ushered Jemma into the overburdened sitting room. Every inch of space was filled with antiques covered with doilies and bric-a-brac. Jemma's memory soared back to her childhood, when she had visited her great-aunt Bernice's home and was intrigued by the abundant clutter of treasures. A deep longing washed over her. *Home.* She had none.

"Sit, please," Abby said.

Since this wasn't a social call, discomfort vied with Jemma's innate sociability. Should she state her business or sink into the huge overstuffed chair covered by an orange-and-brown knitted afghan?

Finding the latter easier, she sank as a cloud of dust rose from the thick chair arms and danced in the sunlight.

Without a word, Abby scurried from the room, then returned followed by Sissy, who was carrying a silver tray discolored with tarnish but obviously an object of pride.

Sissy spread the tea things on the low table, then drew a chair so close to Jemma's side that she felt the woman's knees press against hers. Dumbfounded, she sipped tea and listened to the sisters banter and ply her with questions. Where had Jemma lived previously? Did she have a husband? Children? Why had she moved to Loving?

When they learned that Philip Somerville was Claire's relative, they edged even closer, asked more questions—but Jemma couldn't help them. She didn't know how his wife died. In fact, she hadn't realized he'd been married, at least not that she recalled. And where was his brother Andrew? That question tugged at her own curiosity.

Finally, Jemma sidestepped their questions with one of her own. "I was wondering about your monthly rate…for a boarder,'' she said, then thought better of it. ''Not a boarder, exactly, but someone who might like to stay at the bed and breakfast for a while. A weekly fee, maybe.''

Two sets of eyebrows lifted above widened eyes. Sissy was the first to break her stare by turning to her sister. ''What do we say, Abby?''

Abby paused, and Jemma could almost hear the sound of gears creaking in the woman's head. Obviously, the question surprised her.

''We've had guests stay a week,'' she said finally. ''Our rate is usually fifty dollars a night, which includes breakfast. The rooms have fireplaces and—''

''Fifty.'' Jemma crumbled against the chair back.

Sissy's face shriveled with concern. ''Oh, a weekly rate's less. Much less. Isn't it, sister?''

Abby straightened her back. ''Certainly. I think two hundred and fifty—''

Sissy's elbow swung out, nipping her sister's arm. ''I meant two hundred,'' Abby corrected.

Two pairs of eyes latched to Jemma's, as her hope fluttered into the air like the chair's powdery dust particles. Even two hundred dollars a week was more than she could afford. Far more.

She'd been foolish to think that the Loving Arms might be a short-term haven until she found something else. A new job, first, then an apartment—that was what she needed. Jemma stared down at her feet. She needed to stand on them. Small feet, yes, but they were sturdy and dependable. All she needed was faith.

When she lifted her head, an amusing reality settled into her mind. Living with the Hartmann sisters would be as jumbled and unpredictable as living with Claire. And she loved Claire.

In the momentary silence, Sissy let out a gasp.

Both women turned to her with concern.

"What about Mrs. Dorchester?" Sissy said.

Jemma waited, wondering where Sissy was headed. Who was Mrs. Dorchester?

Abby's face registered interest. Her eyebrows lifted, followed by a slow nod. "It's a possibility," she said.

Like two sleuths solving a case, the sisters settled on a possible solution. Jemma wished she were in on the conversation. They seemed to have a connected thread of thought and their unspoken bond made Jemma feel like an interloper.

Sissy pressed her fingers against Jemma's forearm. "The room is for you, am I correct, dear?"

Jemma nodded, wishing she could have been more subtle. She could almost picture the sisters darting from the house after she left and flying to the boutique to discuss the situation with Claire. No more delay. Jemma *had* to talk with Claire.

"We know of a position," Abby said.

Jemma waited for a clue.

"It's a live-in situation at the Dorchesters'," Sissy added.

A live-in position. Jemma tossed the thought through her mind. This could be what she needed. "What type of work is it?"

"Poor Mrs. Dorchester's mother is ill," Abby said, "and she needs someone to care for her."

"I think there's housework, too," Sissy whispered as if she hated to mention the nasty word.

Jemma let the idea settle. A housekeeping job wasn't exactly what she had in mind, but if it came with a room, it could work. At least, temporarily. She'd clung too long to Claire's skirts. She needed to prove she could survive on her own.

The sisters' chatter continued with stories about Mrs. Dorchester and her mother. With nonchalance, Jemma rose and inched her way to the door. When her feet hit the sidewalk, she had second thoughts about the Dorchesters and headed for the newsstand. Maybe today a suitable position would be in the want ads.

She had to be honest with Claire and tell her what she intended. No more sneaking around like a naughty child. Time she took control. Control? She lowered her eyelids and Philip's handsome face rose behind them. Definitely, she needed control.

Chapter Three

Watching Claire's forlorn face after she broke her news, Jemma had been prodded to call Philip. She had needed someone to talk with and he seemed the logical person. Since she'd told Claire about her plan, she'd felt her mother-in-law's quiet withdrawal. She prayed that once Claire understood, she would know that Jemma's move was for the best.

Jemma had struggled with indecision. Finally she called Mrs. Dorchester. After the interview, Jemma had more concerns, but she'd already accepted the position and didn't want to disappoint the woman. Facing the new job, she needed reassurance that she'd done the right thing.

After telephoning Philip, Jemma tried to relax. Though he'd been slow to agree, he promised to meet her for coffee later in the day. She wondered about his hesitation but dismissed it, knowing he was busy.

To avoid Claire's sad demeanor, Jemma pulled out the new boxes of stock and filled the shelves. She glanced periodically at the clock, watching the time drag.

By three o'clock Jemma was ready to leave. She'd winced, watching Claire drop the price on a leather handbag so low that she was sure it barely covered the cost. Besides that, Claire had given a customer a free brooch, one the customer had admired, with the sale of a silk scarf. Jemma could only shake her head.

Philip was waiting for her at the coffee shop as he'd promised. When she approached him, unbidden tears flooded her eyes. Blinking them back, Jemma caved into the chair beside him.

"What's wrong?" Philip asked, his face filled with concern.

Jemma spilled out her story, a mixture of her new job and her concern for Claire.

"I wish you'd talked with me," he said.

She lifted her head to his direct gaze. "What do you mean?"

He paused, running his fingers through his hair. "First, I think you'll be unhappy with the Dorchesters."

"Why," she asked, "because I'm a housekeeper?" But she already guessed his answer. During the interview, Stacy Dorchester had seemed pompous and mildly demeaning.

"There's nothing wrong with being a housekeeper if you're working for people who value you and think of you as family." He lifted the coffee mug and took a sip before continuing. "I know Stacy and Rod Dorchester. I don't think that will happen."

Jemma didn't think so, either. "But I've already accepted the position."

He stared at his cup, pivoting it right then left against the saucer. "I know. I wish you'd talked with me first." He raised his eyes. "I could have given you a good job, Jemma."

"I know, but I'm tired of living off people." Tears welled in her eyes again, and she brushed them with her fingertips to keep them from trailing down her cheeks. "Claire's been so good to me. Now you. I have no self-respect or self-confidence. I need to stand on my own two feet."

Philip caught her hand in his and brushed the moisture from her fingertips. "Employment at Bay Breeze is self-respecting. I didn't plan to make you a manager, Jemma. I offered you a job. If it's not you, I'll hire someone else. I have a business to run."

The warmth from his touch traveled up her arm. He didn't release her fingers but held her there, his thumb brushing the back of her hand in a soothing caress.

"I'm sorry," she said. A deep sigh shivered through her. "Maybe I'm feeling sorry for myself."

"I doubt it. Everyone wants to be independent. Please understand that I'll be here when and if you need me, Jemma…as a friend…or if you prefer, family. I care about you."

"I'm a shirttail relative. You really don't have to claim me."

He tilted her chin upward with his free fingers. The look in his eyes sent gooseflesh down her arm.

"Would anyone avoid claiming someone so special?"

Someone so special. The words rattled in her head.

He withdrew his hand from her face while his gaze again captured hers. "I don't think you know how lovely you are."

Confusion filled her. She couldn't speak, unable to think of a proper response and fearful that she would infer too much meaning from his words. "Thank you," she said finally.

She sounded weak and ungrateful, but she feared saying more. Hoping more.

"And don't worry about Claire's mood. She loves you. This is just part of her drama. Claire needs to be loved and needed, too."

"I do love her. I'll always be grateful."

"Then, talk with her. Tell her that you need to stand on your own. Let her know that you love her and that you'll be there for her no matter where you live. That's all she wants to hear."

"You think so?"

"I'm sure."

Jemma tendered his words against her heart. Hurting Claire was the last thing she wanted to do.

Philip fell back against the chair, his fingers slipping away from her hand. "Now the other business—'' He released a puff of air and his chin dropped downward.

Jemma shifted gears. "You mean the boutique?"

He nodded. "I suppose I was naive to think that Claire had changed. She has a flair that could make the shop a success…that is, if she doesn't give everything away. I need to talk with her."

Jemma stiffened. "But she'll know that I told you."

"I can be subtle. Don't worry. I'll handle it."

He could handle about anything, she was sure. Jemma leaned back and studied him. He was fifty. She'd discovered his age at the birthday dinner. Fifty had seemed old a few years earlier, but seemed younger now. And maturity looked good—wonderful—on Philip.

His silver-flecked hair against his tanned skin made him the most handsome man she knew. The crinkle lines at his eyes gave him character. His amusement with her…and his gentleness kindled a warmth deep in her heart—like coming home.

A dart of fear shivered through Jemma. She had to stop her imagination from creating cozy, loving images. The man was being kind, just as he'd been kind to Claire. She straightened her back, pushing the warmer thoughts into the distant corners of her mind. Philip probably figured she was helpless and naive. Definitely not someone that he could respect or want to—

"Are you okay?" Philip asked.

She lifted her gaze and witnessed the gentle look in his eyes. She nodded. "A little frightened, I guess."

"It's time you learn to live, Jemma. Don't be frightened. Be adventurous. Open your arms and fly."

He'd put her thoughts into words. If she took one small step into the unknown, who knows what life might offer her?

Philip lay his hand against the clenched fist with which she hugged the table, then looked deeply into her eyes.

She wondered if he could read her mind.

After the shop closed, Philip sat across from Claire in her apartment with the account books spread open on the table. Her profit margin was nonexistent. He'd expected that for a new business. But he'd patiently reviewed the books with her, and he hoped she understood.

"I know you're a generous woman, Claire. You like to show your appreciation to the customer. But you can't give away the merchandise. You need to do something."

Philip jumped when Bodkin leaped from the floor and slid to a landing in the middle of the ledger. The cat gave Philip a haughty gaze and curled up on Claire's penned accounts. "You need to get yourself a computer, Claire." Teasing, he gave Bodkin an evil eye, stroked his fur and dropped the cat to the floor.

"He likes to be in on things," Claire said, reaching down and petting the insulted cat.

Philip delved back in his thoughts to where he'd been before the dive-bombing occurred. "How about…a monthly drawing."

"A drawing?" Slighting Bodkin, Claire straightened her back and gave him an uncertain look.

"Sure. Each customer can drop a card with her name into a fishbowl. You can display the prize. A scarf, let's say, or even a ten-dollar gift certificate."

Claire's face brightened. "I like it. Not a leather handbag. An inexpensive item."

"Right," Philip said, pleased that she caught the idea. "They'll come back more often so they can get their name into the fishbowl and for the opportunity to win a free gift."

Her face showed her pleasure, and he prayed she followed his advice. The summer tourist season had arrived, and the next months could make or break the boutique. Claire needed to understand the situation.

When she smiled, a second lecture made its way to Philip's mouth. "And what about those teeth in your pocket, Claire. Why haven't you seen Doctor Barrow?"

She shook her head. "Because I knew you'd tell him not to charge me. You've done enough. No handouts."

"All right, I promise," he said.

Her words took him back to his conversation with

Jemma the day in the coffee shop. He'd hesitated when she asked for his help. Though he was pleased that she wanted his advice, her request made him wonder. Did she consider him as a friend...a relative? He drew in a ragged breath. *Or a father?* The word nailed him to the chair. Why did he insist on thinking such a thing?

He pushed away his thoughts and refocused on Claire. "I agree. No handouts."

Apparently satisfied, Claire plucked the dentures from her pocket and pulled off a few strands of lint. She rose and headed to the sink. Philip heard the water running and assumed that she was rinsing them under the tap.

"There," she said, turning around to face him, this time wearing her teeth. "I promise I'll see him. But remember *your* promise. No charity."

Philip agreed again and sank against the chair. He picked up his cola and took a sip. Despite his thoughts of Jemma, Claire tickled him. He'd controlled an earlier grin, but now he allowed himself to smile.

Philip had tried to avoid focusing on her getup— black spandex pants and some sort of off-the-shoulder gypsy blouse. A huge pair of hoop earrings hung from her ears and her arms had enough bangles to ring out the old and ring in the new. If that didn't attract customers, what would?

"You're smiling," Claire said. "I like to see

that." She peered at him. "You're a good-looking man, Philip."

"Thank you. You're unbelievable yourself, Claire." His double meaning broadened his grin. "I'm glad you've cheered up."

Her lightheartedness faded. "Me, too. I'm ashamed of myself. Poor Jemma. I wasn't very nice the last days she was here. Selfishness. That's what it was."

"You, selfish?"

"Me," she said, answering his question. "I was thinking of my own wants. Jemma needs to get on with her life and not worry about her old mother-in-law. She's a young woman who should have—"

She paused, and Philip started to respond, but Claire's eyes brightened and she continued.

"She should have a husband...and a family. That's what she needs," Claire pronounced and leaned forward.

At the mental image of Jemma with a husband and family, Philip froze.

"Maybe a businessman...a *successful* business-man," she continued. "One who can let her stay home with the little ones while he brings home the bacon."

Reeling at what he was feeling, Philip threw his head back and laughed, covering the truth. "I hope you're not thinking of me, Claire. I'm old enough to be her father."

"Baloney!" Claire swished away his comment with her hand.

Philip's chest tightened. Jemma did deserve a happy, fulfilled life—one that was complete, with a loving husband and children. A wave of longing shivered down his back.

"You old? No way," Claire said. "You're just the kind of man Jemma needs. One with a good head on his shoulders. I've lived to regret my son's inability to make that lovely girl happy. Jemma tried to make it work. Tried like a trooper. But you can't be happy living with waste and alcohol…and unfaithfulness. I know."

Philip wanted to stop her. He didn't want to know about Jemma's unhappy existence. Yet…part of him did. Part of him wanted to hold her in his arms, protect and shield her from further hurt. He wanted to make her smile. Wanted to love her. Wanted to start a family with her.

The image sliced through his thoughts while cold fear stabbed his heart. It was impossible. He'd become a role model in the community, a man who worked hard and stuck by his father's dream. Many people looked up to him. How would they perceive him if he were involved with a woman almost half his age. *Cradle robber.* That's what they'd call him. He'd heard the term before. Snide comments behind people's backs. Why did he care what people thought? People would scorn him…but worse, they'd ridicule Jemma. He couldn't allow that.

Straightening his back, Philip closed the ledger. "I'm serious about a computer, Claire. You could use a spreadsheet program and keep your records much more easily than you're doing now." He rose. "And no math."

"No math? How's that?"

"The program figures it for you. Give that some thought." His mind wandered as he noticed a stack of photographs on a side table. He lifted the stack and felt his heart give a kick when Jemma's smiling face glowed from one of the photos.

He grinned. Apparently for posterity, Claire had taken photos of every nook and cranny and every angle of the store. She'd snapped Jemma dressing the storefront window, Jemma setting up a table display. Jemma had only taken a few pictures of Claire.

"Nice photos, huh?" Claire leaned over his shoulder. "I'm keeping a scrapbook."

"Yes, they're great." His gaze lingered on one lovely photograph of Jemma. "This is an excellent shot."

"Keep it," she said.

Though he longed to, he shook his head. "What about your scrapbook?"

"This one's nice of her," Claire said, fingering through the photos. "Take a couple."

Philip smiled, recognizing Claire's desire to please the world. He was glad he hadn't mentioned he liked her shoes. He'd be carrying them home in a paper sack. "No, no, they're yours, Claire. Really."

She finally stopped pushing, and he quickly said goodbye before he forgot and mentioned he liked something else of hers. With a wave, he escaped down the stairs, and at the bottom slipped his hand into his jacket pocket for the keys.

He stopped and glanced back up the stairs, expecting to see Claire's smiling face. She wasn't there. Somehow she'd put something in his pocket when he wasn't paying attention.

Delving deeper, he drew out Claire's gift. His chest tightened as he eyed one photo after another—each one of Jemma's smiling face.

"Claire, what are you doing to me?"

The answer came from his heart. She'd done nothing. The problem was his. He lowered his eyes to one of the photographs and faced the truth. He was the one out of control.

In her small bedroom, Jemma tugged pantyhose up her legs, then rose and pulled a slip over her head. Moving to the mirror, she held the summer dress in front of her, hoping that the yellow print didn't make her look too pale. It had been on sale and she couldn't pass up the bargain.

Since moving into the Dorchesters' residence, Jemma felt like a prisoner. The couple were tolerable, but demanding. Jemma had known when she accepted the job that the work wouldn't be easy. She was used to hard work. But at the Dorchesters', no matter how hard she tried, she was chastised for the smallest mistake—while they seemed to ignore her efforts.

She looked toward heaven, asking God to forgive her. Gratitude was not a guarantee in life. Her reward would be in heaven. Rod Dorchester's vile language made Jemma cringe each time she heard the Lord's name in vain. Yet she'd grown fond of Stacy Dorchester's elderly mother, for whom she cared. She wondered how long she could cope with the situation.

But her life had a bright side. Claire had made every effort to let Jemma know that all was forgiven, and from what she could tell, Philip had done an excellent job of explaining things to Claire. The monthly drawing idea was a hit and even tourists participated, leaving their address and hoping to win the colorful scarf Claire displayed as the prize.

But Philip? She hadn't seen him for the past three weeks.

Her chest tightened, knowing tonight they'd be together. He'd called and invited her to join him and Claire for the make-up birthday dinner. One without interruptions. She missed him more than she wanted to admit.

Philip was not only a good businessman. He seemed to understand human nature. He'd helped her with Claire and guided Claire to think in a more businesslike manner. And he'd even guessed she would dislike her work with the Dorchesters. Had he known about Mr. Dorchester's cursing?

Jemma dropped the dress over her head and studied herself in the mirror. Was it the dress or her hair she didn't like? She grabbed a clasp, pulled her curls away from her face and secured it. A few wispy strands escaped. With the whisk of a facial brush, she added color to her cheeks and daubed on a bright lipstick. She'd pass.

She slipped on her lowest strap heels, grabbed her shoulder bag and hurried down the back steps. She'd agreed to wait for Philip and Claire out front, wanting no part of the Dorchesters' curious stares.

Late afternoon sun filtered through the trees, spreading dark and light patterns on the ground that shifted and flickered with the breeze. She usually loved summer: it held promise of bright skies and warm days. But this summer left her feeling cheated. She barely had time to enjoy a moment of relaxation, let alone the outdoors.

Her one day off seemed to fly. And though her nights were free, the Dorchesters' social calendar left Jemma in charge of the elderly woman many evenings. Grandma Agnes enjoyed her company, and Jemma couldn't disappoint her.

Jemma headed down the block, away from the austere brick house. A neighbor's rose garden sent its rich fragrance sailing on the air, and Jemma stopped, filling her lungs with the aroma that reminded her of Philip's aftershave.

When an automobile turned the corner, Jemma recognized Philip's car, and anticipation jarred her senses. During the past weeks, she'd lived for this day—to see him again and enjoy his company.

Through the windshield, she could see his silhouette etched by the lowering sun. Her heart skipped. She forgot to breathe. She wanted to stamp her foot at her foolishness.

When he pulled to the curb beside her, Philip leaned over and pushed open the passenger door. She stepped forward, glancing into the back seat to greet Claire.

The seat was empty.

Philip answered her question before she asked. "Claire begged to be excused. She said she was tired and felt a cold coming on."

Jemma knew better. Claire was being Claire. She'd hinted to Jemma when they visited her last that Philip would make a wonderful husband...for someone.

Since she'd found no point in arguing with Claire, Jemma had agreed. For someone, Philip would make a wonderful husband. But the *someone* wasn't her.

Jemma wanted to be aggravated, but this was Claire's way. Tonight Claire had generously given up a nice dinner to arrange this private rendezvous.

Claire's manipulation made Jemma feel ill at ease. Still, she could do nothing now, so she slid into the passenger seat, closed the door and gathered her thoughts before facing Philip.

"I suppose I should have let you know Claire wasn't coming," he said. "I hope you don't mind."

She avoided his eyes. "I'm just surprised."

"We could call it off and wait until she's feeling better."

Call it off? If he did, Jemma would be terribly disappointed. If he didn't, they would spend the evening together and Jemma would spend the night fighting her foolish longings. "Is that what you'd like to do?" Jemma asked, shuffling through her conflicting emotions.

"Not at all," he said, his voice soft and deep.

She faced him, afraid to look in his eyes, but she did. "Then, I'd enjoy having dinner with you."

He smiled. "I'm glad."

They drove in silence except for an occasional comment about the scenery or the day. In a short time they reached the inn's parking lot.

Surrounded by large elms, the Inn on Spring Lake was a low, rambling stone building that sat on the edge of a rise overlooking the lake that eventually flowed into nearby Lake Michigan.

They were guided to a cozy table beside a window that looked out on the calm, bottle-green water. Afraid to look directly into Philip's eyes, Jemma stared out at the landscape. Gulls soared and dipped, searching for their evening meal, and when the birds touched the silent water, concentric ripples rolled outward, tipped in gold from the setting sun.

Occasionally, Jemma gave Philip a sidelong glance, but his gaze seemed focused on her. The admiring look stirred her imagination.

"I'm always amazed at how quickly the sun goes down," Jemma said, watching the golden orb touch the water, sending quicksilver arrows darting across the blue stillness. "Time is a strange phenomenon."

With a questioning look, Philip tilted his head.

"If you're happy, time flies...like this glorious sun. In the blink of an eye, it vanishes into night and returns as another fleeting day. But when you're lonely or miserable, it drags like a funeral dirge. Unending."

"I don't want you to be miserable, Jemma. Tell me you're not." He moved his hand across the tabletop and rested it on hers.

His touch wrapped her in an unexpected calm. "Not miserable, exactly. But far from where I'd like to be."

"And where would you like to be?"

She longed to tell him. She'd like to be close to him, protected in his strong arms and soothed with his deep, reassuring voice. "I don't know," she answered finally. "But not at the Dorchesters."

"Then, resign."

It was as simple as that. *Resign.* She pondered the thought. She could easily give her notice—give them time to replace her—but she wasn't one to act rashly. "What would I do then? Go back to Claire's?" She lowered her eyes. "I can't. I really can't."

"I have a job waiting for you. Believe me, you can take your pick. Reservation desk, office clerk, waitress, housekeeper. You're doing that now. A job at Bay Breeze would be much better…and I guarantee a better wage.''

She needed to think. Even more, she needed to ask God what to do. ''I don't know. I just can't—''

He pressed his finger to her lips, then turned her head with his free hand.

She looked through the window and witnessed a lake of fire and diamonds. A miracle of orange, gold and silver spread across the water in glinting prisms of refracted light. A gasp escaped her.

''So beautiful,'' Philip whispered.

''It is,'' she whispered. She returned her gaze to his and felt her head spin, seeing his tender, telling smile.

''The sunset, too, Jemma, but I'm talking about you. You're like a spring day…all fresh and glowing with your golden hair and dress covered with sprigs of flowers.''

He touched the sleeve of her simple print gown, sending a shiver of excitement down her arm.

''So young…and expectant. I envy you. I wish I was young again.''

''You envy me?'' Jemma stared at him with disbelief. ''Me?'' She shook her head. ''Anyone would envy you. You have everything a person could want. Success, wealth, generosity, kindness, people who look up to you—''

''I have nothing.''

She stopped breathing.

''Don't look at me like that. I'm not out of my

mind. My life is set. No adventure. No surprises. No family.''

Her mind shot back to their first birthday dinner. ''Your brother?''

''No. Not that kind of family. A family of my own.''

Jemma couldn't believe what she heard. ''A while ago you told me to spread my arms and fly. How about taking your own advice?''

''My own advice is for the young. I'm old enough to be your father, Jemma. Could you see your father spreading his arms and flying?''

''He could be...in heaven. My father died years ago.''

His face blanched. ''I'm sorry. I didn't know.''

''That's okay—but don't you see? You're only fifty. That's still young enough for—''

''Not for what I want.''

Like a whirlwind, questions spun through Jemma's mind. What did he want? Not her, that was clear. Was there some woman in his life? A woman he loved who didn't love him? How could that be? She had no words, no answers that rose from the gale in her head.

She turned and faced the water, seeing the last of the golden rays spill across the horizon, the heavens shadowing to coral and violet. Like her dreams, the sky had glowed, then faded to nothing but black night.

One stark thought pierced the darkness. She could never work at Bay Breeze. Seeing Philip every day would weigh on her heart. And she'd already had enough sorrow for a whole lifetime.

Chapter Four

"I understand," Philip said, controlling his discouragement. "I've heard the complaints myself."

Ian Barry fiddled with the keys clutched in his hand and shuffled from one foot to the other. "You're the boss, Philip, but I'm getting nailed every day for the positions we haven't filled."

"I know." Philip's focus riveted to the telephone. Why hadn't Jemma called and accepted his job offer? He knew the time had come when he could no longer avoid filling the resort's needs. He'd held open two particular jobs that he thought Jemma would enjoy.

Ian scowled at the wad of keys and dropped them into his suit jacket pocket. "We're heading for the prime tourist season and—"

"Have Personnel fill the slots, Ian. I hear you," Philip said, monitoring the stress in his voice.

"If I understood why we've waited so long, I'd—"

"Ian," Philip said, rising, "I said notify Personnel to process the applications. You'll have all the help you need in a couple of days."

Ian adjusted his eyeglass frames and nodded. "All right, then." With a final puzzled look, he strode from the office and closed the door.

Sinking into his chair, Philip shut his eyes. He had no other option. Now if Jemma wanted a job, he would have little to offer except a lower paying position like housekeeping. Why was Jemma so headstrong?

Philip swiveled his high-backed chair to face the window and Lake Michigan glinting in the late afternoon sun. In the distance, he watched resort guests lolling on the beach or standing on the pier enjoying the scenery. The tennis courts and golf tee-times were booked throughout the day, and in the evening, the resort restaurants had nearly reached capacity seating. Philip was awed that God had blessed him so abundantly.

But why him? What happened to God's blessings for his brother, Andrew? From the same parental seed, Philip and Andrew were so different. His brother had been bored with the resort and longed for adventure and freedom, while Philip had stayed by his father's side and learned the business. By the time his father retired and later died, Philip had been experienced and well-trained in handling the resort. But Andrew…?

Guilt weighed heavily on Philip's shoulders. His brother had not faired as well—and now what? What would he do if Andrew returned? Philip had sensed something in their telephone conversation a few weeks earlier, as if Andrew wanted forgiveness for breaking his father's heart, for squandering his share of the family fortune, for walking away from everyone who loved him.

Philip would never understand that driving need for independence. Take Jemma. She'd rejected his offer. But why? Was it really a desire for this freedom Philip didn't understand, or was she rejecting *him?* He wondered if she sensed he cared too much.

Refocusing on the lake, Philip watched the waves roll in. Hitting the shore, they dragged the sand back to sea, leaving debris behind in their wake. The symbolism smacked him. Did Jemma see him as dashing into her life and knocking her off balance? *I need to stand on my own two feet,* she'd said. Did she fear he would leave her floundering in the debris of his helpfulness?

Before he could think the question through, the telephone jolted him to action. He grabbed the receiver and, following his greeting, heard Claire's exuberant voice.

"Philip, where have you been?"

"Busy, Claire." He felt guilt over his neglect. "The first weeks of the tourist season are always like this." He rolled his shoulders in an attempt to dispel the tension. "How are things with you? No problems, I hope."

"I'm great. Miss hearing from you, that's all. I wondered if you'd like to drop by tonight for dinner. I'm making something you like."

Her offer sent a buzz of thoughts whirring through his mind. With so many nit-picking details, he'd planned to stay in the office late that evening. Still, how could he refuse? "Give me a hint? What would I miss?"

"You'll have to come and see," she said, her voice teasing. "Any time that's good for you, Philip."

Philip eyed the wall clock. "How about eight, Claire?" With the late hour, he hoped for a counteroffer, a rain check for another day.

"Great," she said. "See you then."

When he hung up, Philip accepted that his ploy hadn't worked. Yet, as well as a good meal, another positive side of the invitation came to him. Claire might tell him how Jemma had faired the past weeks. Was Jemma avoiding him?

As she dressed for dinner, Jemma's cheeks burned with humiliation and anger. She'd willingly given up the past two evenings to stay with Agnes, but today when she had plans of her own, Rod Dorchester had upbraided her—using the Lord's name—for her unwillingness to spend another night caring for his mother-in-law. Had he asked her before Claire's call, Jemma would have honored his request.

As Jemma slipped a knit top over her head, she wondered what God would have her do. Being in a subservient position, she felt unable to say anything about her employer's sinful language. How much longer could she bear it?

Feeling no need to fuss over her appearance, Jemma splotched on fresh lipstick and clipped her unruly curls into a ponytail. Claire had seen her looking much worse, so what did it matter? She hurried down the back stairs, out the side gate and along the sidewalk toward Loving Treasures.

In the back of her mind, Jemma wondered why Claire had called in the afternoon to invite her to dinner so late, but she tossed it off to Claire's incomprehensible abandon. In the blink of an eye, Claire reached out to whatever struck her fancy.

When the telephone had rung earlier, Jemma hoped to hear Philip's voice. Weeks had passed since they'd been together and Jemma missed his warmth and good humor—even though seeing him made her pulse race. Why did she react so foolishly? Philip was a respected man. He didn't need a poor shop girl clinging to his side for support. Besides, she wanted independence.

In the early evening breeze, Jemma breathed in a mixture of scents—summer flowers, dusty cement, and an occasional whiff of lake air drifting from the

Grand River that emptied into Lake Michigan only a couple of miles away.

Reaching Claire's shop, Jemma took the side entrance. As soon as she opened the outer door, the rich scent of roast beef roused her taste buds. Curious why Claire would choose a warm summer day to make a roast, Jemma hurried up the stairs and, with a single tap, pushed open the door.

"Smells wonderful, Claire," she said, stepping into the kitchen and witnessing Claire's latest fashion statement: a floral magenta caftan.

"It's the rosemary," Claire said. "Rosemary and pork, rosemary and beef—they go together like love and marriage." As the analogy left her mouth, a grin shot to Claire's face. "Bad example," she said. "How about Cupid and his arrows?"

Puzzled, Jemma stood for a moment wondering about Claire's analogies. They both had a smattering of romance.

"I'm curious, Claire," Jemma asked, "why are you making such a fancy dinner?"

"It was an inspiration."

Inspiration? Jemma narrowed her eyes, studying Claire as she busied herself at the stove. Without questioning further, Jemma shifted her focus to the small table and counted three plates.

She understood. Claire had met someone.

But that surprised her. Although Claire had been widowed for years, her mother-in-law had vowed she would never again allow a man in her life. Jemma had believed her. No man had ever appeared to catch Claire's eye. Yet, Jemma hoped someday Claire would find love. Single life could be lonely.

Rather than ruin Claire's surprise, Jemma veered the conversation in another direction. "May I help you?"

"No, I'm about finished," she said, her long, pointed sleeve barely escaping a simmering pan on the stove. "I put the Yorkshire pudding in the oven just before you arrived."

Hearing her statement, Jemma realized that Claire meant business. Yorkshire pudding was one of Claire's specialities for important occasions. Puzzled, Jemma eyed the older woman. Why hadn't she heard about this romance before?

Claire swung away from the stove, her caftan billowing around her ankles. "Let's sit in the living room and talk." She headed toward the doorway and beckoned Jemma to follow.

Chuckling to herself, Jemma was sure the *talk* would be the older woman's romantic confession.

Claire sat in an easy chair and gestured toward the sofa. Jemma sank into the soft cushions and waited.

"Tell me about your work," Claire said.

Her question threw Jemma off-kilter.

"Are things any better?" Claire asked, a sincere look settling on her face.

Not wanting to ruin the evening with her distress, Jemma gave Claire a sketchy picture of her week and dwelt on her enjoyment of spending time with the elderly Agnes. She sensed that Claire was bursting with questions, but before Claire could prod Jemma for more details, the doorbell rang and Jemma breathed a relieved sigh. Her mother-in-law had an amazing knack for dragging the truth out of her.

Claire sent Jemma an unsettling look and rose, while the cat appeared out of nowhere to follow her. Without comment, she sailed toward the side door. Jemma listened and heard the murmur of a masculine voice drowned beneath Claire's exuberant welcome.

Curious, Jemma watched the doorway for her first glimpse of Claire's friend. When the man strolled through the archway, Jemma gasped. "Philip!"

"Jemma?"

The simultaneous acknowledgments made it clear that neither had known of the other's attendance.

"Claire didn't tell me," Philip said, hesitating in the middle of the room.

His surprised face sent her heart sinking.

"Sit, Philip," Claire said. "The sofa's most comfortable." She breezed past him and wafted her flowing sleeve in Jemma's direction.

As Philip studied the empty space beside Jemma, Claire sank into the lone chair.

Regaining her breath, Jemma shifted closer to the arm. Obviously Philip wouldn't have come had he known she'd been invited. Jemma noted the surprise in his voice and the discomfort in his expression.

"Isn't this nice," Claire said, ignoring the tension

that filled the room. "I'm pleased you could both come on such short notice."

Philip edged forward. "I smelled the roast beef when I came in, Claire. Don't tell me you're making…"

"Yorkshire pudding," she said, ending his question. "Your favorite."

"It is," he said, settling onto the sofa beside Jemma. "I haven't had that in years."

"You mentioned my pot roast one day in the shop," she said.

"Yes, I did…and the Yorkshire pudding. It's been years since I had it."

Claire laughed. "It will be years longer, unless I finish up." She rose and swept toward the kitchen.

Jemma seized the moment and rose. "Let me help, Claire."

But before she could take a step, Claire shooed her back. "You and Philip talk. Everything will be ready in a minute."

As the command left Claire's mouth, Jemma saw the picture as clearly as a summer sky. The romance Claire was celebrating was one she'd contrived. Jemma and Philip's. No wonder Claire hadn't said a word about a new man in her life.

Rattled by the awareness, Jemma pivoted to face Philip. "How have you been?" she asked, sitting as close as she could to the sofa arm.

"Busy. Too busy," he said. "I've wanted to call and see how—"

His excuse settled on Jemma's ear. "Don't apologize, please. I know your life is very complicated. Mine is, well, is quieter. Much more..." She couldn't find the word. Simple? No, it was horrible.

Philip shifted and rested his hand on her arm. "To be honest, I'd hoped that you would call."

She'd wished the same. But he hadn't. "Me?"

He shrugged. "Well, besides missing your friendship, I hoped you'd change your mind about the job."

Hearing his offer again, Jemma longed to give in and accept. Her heart thudded at the thought of telling him about Mr. Dorchester's language and her unhappiness. But as she gathered courage, Claire appeared in the doorway, calling them to dinner.

Hearing Claire's invitation, Philip drew in a deep breath, savoring the appetizing aroma that followed her into the room. He rose, and before he could be a gentleman, Jemma popped up and darted away as if her life had been threatened. Her reaction set him on edge.

Though the table was small, Claire filled it with roast beef and potatoes, boiled carrots, and great slabs of the pudding. Philip drenched the meal in thick, brown gravy.

As they concentrated on their food, conversation dwindled, and when they'd finished, Philip congratulated Claire on her culinary skills. Before he or Jemma could volunteer to help with the clean-up, she directed them back to the living room, leaving Claire to deal with a meowing Bodkin.

"Go. Go," Claire said, chasing them away. "When I'm finished here, I'll bring in coffee and dessert."

Her eagerness aroused his curiosity, but now he could take advantage of his time alone with Jemma. In a rare quiet moment during the meal, Philip had pondered how he would question Jemma. He longed to know what had upset her, and decided a direct approach was necessary.

Jemma left the kitchen, and Philip followed. Before she could sink into the farthest corner of the sofa, he captured her arm. "What is it, Jemma? Have I upset you in some way?"

"No. No, you haven't done anything."

Her arm stiffened beneath his hand.

"You're not being truthful," Philip said. "Please tell me what I've done."

A look of defeat settled on her face and she sank onto the sofa. "It's me, Philip. You've made me a job offer, and I've refused because I want to help myself instead of having everyone bail me out of my troubles. I already told you that." A look of panic filled her eyes. "But I'm very disturbed about my current job…and I really need some advice."

Sitting beside her, he slipped his arm comfortingly around her shoulder. "What is it? Tell me."

As if he'd opened the floodgates, Jemma poured out her story—her efforts to make the family happy, her pleasure in tending to Agnes, yet her overwhelming misery at Rod's scolding and cursing.

Tears filled her eyes, and Philip glanced at the doorway, hoping he had time to respond before Claire flew into the room. "Look, Jemma, you have to speak your mind. Tell Rod that you're a Christian and you're offended by his cursing."

"But I'm his employee and—"

"Jemma, this isn't the dark ages. Employees have rights. Don't you think I'd be sitting in court if I harassed one of my workers?"

She wiped the escaping tears from her eyes. "Yes, but—"

"But nothing. Tomorrow, talk with him. I'm sure he'll understand and make an effort to control his language."

Except that Philip wasn't sure, and the more he thought about the situation, the more he wondered if his advice might cause Jemma more problems. He'd had an occasional conversation with Rod that had left him amazed at the man's poor reasoning.

When he focused on Jemma's calmed expression, Philip didn't have the heart to retract his suggestion. Beneath his embrace, the tension had left her shoulders and her posture seemed more relaxed. Now, all he could do was pray he hadn't misguided her.

Jemma stood in her tiny bedroom and stared at her opened suitcase, amazed at how badly her request had been received. Rod Dorchester had given her no ultimatum. A housekeeper should not question his authority, he'd said, nor criticize his choice of words. She had resigned.

Placing a blouse on the bed, Jemma smoothed it and folded each sleeve, wondering if she'd done the right thing. With Claire busy in the store, the only person she could think of to help her was Philip. When she called, he responded immediately and said he would be right there.

Two boxes were piled by the door, and Jemma had one more suitcase to pack. If her possessions weren't so cumbersome, she would have called a taxi rather than ask Philip for help.

Though Philip apologized and blamed himself for her situation, Jemma felt differently. His advice had been the only solution. Staying there and accepting Mr. Dorchester's vile language would have gone against Jemma's principles and her faith. She had to leave. God would have had her do the same, she was sure.

From her open window, Jemma heard wheels crunch against the cement driveway. She glanced out the window and watched Philip exit the car and head toward the back door.

Jemma hurried down the stairs. When she opened the door, her emotions took command and she fell into his arms. Philip's voice wrapped around her like a warm blanket on a cold night. He soothed her with his words and calmed her with his presence.

When she gained control, she steered him up the

staircase to her room, and together they toted her
belongings to the car. Philip loaded his trunk while
Jemma settled into the passenger seat. For the first
time in weeks, she felt a tremendous weight lift from
her shoulders.

"Jemma," Philip said, sliding in beside her. "I
feel responsible for this. I had second thoughts after
we talked, but I hoped Rod would use common sense
and take your request to heart." He ran his hand
along her cheek. "But I'm not sure he has one."

Puzzled, Jemma turned her face to his. "Has
one?"

"A heart," Philip said, a tender grin curving his
mouth. He released a sigh. "So where do we go from
here?"

Jemma's pulse lurched. "After I spoke with you,
I called Claire. I'll go back there until I can find a
small place. I've saved a little money. At least I'm
walking away with that."

"Good for you, and you know, if…"

Philip faltered, and Jemma understood. "Thank
you for not offering me money or a free room at the
resort." She shook her head. "Philip, you have a
good heart. A generous heart, but—"

"Shush," he said, caressing the length of her hair.
"You don't need to say a word. I'm trying to respect
your wishes."

She felt pleased that he seemed to understand.

Philip sat bolt upright and smacked his palms
against the steering wheel. "Let's celebrate."

His suggestion came from nowhere, and Jemma looked at him curiously. "Celebrate what?"

"Your freedom from tyranny." He sent her a wry smile.

"What did you have in mind? Apartment hunting?"

"That's tomorrow," he said. "Have you ever sailed, Jemma?"

"Sailed?"

"In a boat? On the water?"

She laughed. "I know what sailing is. I was just surprised."

"Well...have you?"

"No, I've never sailed. I've never done a lot of things that people take for granted. I'm embarrassed at my naiveté."

He shook his head. "Don't be embarrassed. Your inexperience will give me the fun of sharing some new things with you."

"Do you rent boats at the marina in town?"

Philip released a full-bodied laugh. "No need to rent, Jemma. I own a sailboat. It's moored at the resort."

Jemma felt a flush heat her face. Talk about naive—she'd win the prize. A man in Philip's shoes would own a sailboat. Possibly even a whole fleet of sailboats.

When Philip turned the key in the ignition, Jemma focused outside the window, struggling with her anxiety. She closed her eyes, imagining the wind in the sails and Philips strong hands at the wheel.

Jemma leaned against the seat cushions, enjoying the sun warming her arms while the breeze ruffled her hair. The boat glided over the waves like a bird on the wind, smooth and gentle. Looking over the edge, she watched the lake split at the bow and roll along the side of the boat in billows of white foam. She'd never imagined how it might feel to sail on a summer afternoon.

Philip stood at the helm, looking like a true sailor in his cap, and his navy polo shirt with a white anchor on the pocket, circled by the words Grand Haven Yacht Club. While he faced the bow, Jemma watched him, unnoticed, admiring his muscular arms as he guided the boat over the lake.

Philip told her it was a thirty-five-foot sloop. Whatever it was, she enjoyed every minute of it. Earlier, as they had approached the boat at the peer, she'd been curious about the name printed on the hull. *My Lady.* Later, if she had the nerve, she would ask him what it meant. Had he referred to his wife as "my lady?" She pulled her thoughts away from his wife. She'd died too young, just as Lyle had done.

Occasionally, Philip glanced her way, sending her a smile as warm and stirring as the breeze. When he beckoned, she rose on shaky legs and, holding the railing, moved to his side.

"Would you like to take the wheel?" he asked.

"Me?" In a panic, she shook her head. "I can't."

"Sure you can." He guided her by the elbow and moved her into place.

She gripped the wheel, feeling the power of the vessel gliding over the rolling waves.

"Just keep your eye on the flag." He pointed to the small ensign at the top of the mast, flapping in the wind. "See the way the wind's blowing? Just keep the boat at a forty-five-degree angle to the wind. Use that as your guide."

As her guide? She didn't know exactly what he meant, but Philip seemed confident. She struggled to relax the tension in her back. With an occasional glance at the flag, she looked ahead at a stretch of glistening blue water.

Philip disappeared into the cabin, and Jemma's tension returned. She prayed he wouldn't be long, and felt relieved when he reappeared a moment later. She watched him at the rigging mast, raising a third sail. He was preoccupied, but at least he was back on deck.

Enjoying and yet nervous about her turn at the wheel, Jemma kept her sight aimed at the horizon until she sensed Philip behind her.

"How am I doing?" she asked over the wind.

A low chuckle brushed against her ear. "Do you see the sails flapping all over the place? We're sailing too close to the wind."

"Too close to the wind?" How could she be too

close? Wind was wind. She eyed him over her shoulder to see if he was teasing.

He nodded, his face as serious as a surgeon's. He moved in beside her, taking the wheel with one hand and wrapping the other around her shoulder with a gentle squeeze. "It takes practice. You'll learn."

Was he hinting that he would take her sailing again? She'd learn? What did he mean?

Jemma knew she would remember this wonderful afternoon as one of the best days of her life.

She gave him a feeble smile and worked her way to the safety of the bench. Looking across the vast expanse of blue and green extending to the horizon, she lifted her gaze to the bright, cloudless sky and perceived God's presence. Mountains, ravines, forests, oceans. God created and ruled all nature. He could move mountains. And so could she if she had faith.

Faith? She winced, thinking of her weak conviction. The Bible promised so much, but she wondered if those promises were only for martyrs and prophets, the people of the Bible—people who walked on water and split the sea in two for others to walk on dry land. Reality told her she could never do that.

But Jemma didn't want to work miracles. She only wanted a life that felt complete. A life that had purpose and fulfillment. Was that asking for a miracle?

She leaned back and pondered if the moment was right to question Philip. Or would it ruin their afternoon? She took a deep breath. "May I ask you a couple of personal questions?"

Unmoving, he eyed her. "What do you mean?"

"Just things I've wondered about," she said, realizing that she may have made a mistake.

He sat as if transfixed, then raised his head. "Try me."

Troubled by his reaction, she shuffled her questions, starting with one she hoped was the safest. "Why is the boat named *My Lady?*"

A deep chuckle flew from his chest. "That's the personal question?"

"One of them." She didn't understand his reaction. The question didn't seem at all funny to her.

"Oh, Jemma, I was prepared for something far more…intimate."

Jemma swallowed the gasp that had lodged in her throat. "Intimate? You were?"

"I meant something more private." He looked at the flag high on the mast, then lowered his eyes. "So you've been wondering about *My Lady*. I suppose I figured that after Susan's death the sailboat would be the only other woman in my life."

She hadn't known what to expect, but Jemma had expected something more. "You mean that's it?"

"What did you think?"

She shrugged. "I thought maybe that was a pet name you called your wife. You know, like she's 'my lady.'"

"Sorry if I disappointed you."

But he hadn't. "My Lady" would be a special name for a special woman. Jemma didn't want to think about Philip with any woman...only her. "And my next question—how did Susan die?"

"In surgery. An aneurysm."

"I'm sorry. I know she was young." Without expecting it, Jemma did feel sorry for this unknown woman whose life had been taken so early.

"Susan was only a little older than you are. Life cheated her."

Did he mean life? Or God? If ever a time seemed right, it was now. As the question filled her mind, Jemma held her breath.

"Philip, do you believe in God?"

Chapter Five

Do you believe in God? Philip looked at her, wondering how this fit into their conversation. "That's a strange question."

"Not really. You said that life cheated Susan. I wondered if you meant...God."

He thought back to the moment before he had spoken. Maybe that was what he had meant. Once he'd felt that way. He studied Jemma's anxious expression. "No, I think I meant life."

"Oh," she said with a look of disappointment.

He wondered how she might have reacted if he'd said yes, he meant God. "Isn't life what we make it?"

This time she looked puzzled. "Sure...I guess so."

"We make choices. We have free will to use our lives or put one foot in a rut and go nowhere."

"Is that me? One foot in a rut?"

Philip laughed. "No, Jemma, that would never be you." But it was him. He'd become like Susan. No zeal to live. No hope for the future. One foot in his job and the other...

"But I was like that once," Jemma said, "before I came to Loving. I was a widow. Nothing more, nothing less. Lyle's poor wife. I'll always be grateful to Claire for insisting we take a giant step and move here."

"So will I."

She looked at him with questioning eyes.

Philip knew he'd said too much. If he looked at her gentle face much longer or the soft shapely flesh above her knee, he'd be in trouble.

Unexpectedly, she gave him a silly grin. "I get it. You're pleased because Claire needs your help...and that gives you purpose."

Jolted by her comment, he forced a brief chuckle, then looked ahead at the shoreline on the horizon. She'd hit too close to the truth.

Jemma realized Philip was heading toward shore, and disappointment settled over her. She hated that their lovely day was coming to an end. Back on land, she would have to think about an apartment...and worse, a job.

As the vessel neared the shore, the landscape looked unfamiliar. Jemma leaned forward, scanning the shoreline. The resort was nowhere in sight.

"Where are we?" she asked, moving toward him

while forcing her voice to pierce the thud of waves and the flap of sails.

"Muskegon," he said. "I thought we'd tie up at the marina and have dinner."

"But I'm not dressed for—"

An amused grin settled on Philip's face. "No one dresses for dinner here. You look lovely. Windblown and sun kissed."

His sweet words sent tendrils of yearning down her limbs. No man had ever said such beautiful things to her. Not even Lyle.

With careful steps, she returned to the bench and opened her compact shoulder bag. She pulled out a small oval mirror and eyed herself. Though her hair was a mess, the sun had definitely brightened her cheeks. With a quick dash of her comb, she would have to make the best of it.

As the boat drew closer to shore, Philip lowered the sails while Jemma made a second attempt at aiming the sloop toward shore. With the visual to guide her, she stood bravely at the helm.

Once the sails were stowed, Philip started the motor and steered into the marina.

Jemma watched Philip with admiration as he tied the boat to the pier. He worked with precision, knotting the lines to the moorings. When the vessel was secured, Jemma grabbed her shoulder bag before Philip helped her step to the broad wooden planks. She hesitated a moment, willing her trembling legs to relax.

When she was ready, Philip led the way to the restaurant. After they had placed their orders, Jemma drew in a calming breath, overwhelmed by the day.

"I'm totally at a loss for words," she said, gazing at Philip's sensitive face. "How do I thank you for showing me a world I might never have known?"

"You don't have to Jemma. You're a unique, lovely woman, and it was my pleasure to enjoy your company."

His gentle look sent her heart aflutter. *Love. Unique. Lovely.* Words so foreign to her. Words that captured her imagination and sent her soaring.

"Out there on the lake," he said, "your face beamed with excitement...like a child's."

Her winging spirit took a nosedive. Is that what he thought? She was a child to be entertained? He could take her to the circus. Buy her balloons and cotton candy. Was that all she was to him? Another outlet for his compulsive philanthropy?

Philip's face twisted and he fixed his palm against her forearm. "Jemma, please. I didn't say that you are a child. By no means. You're a woman. A delightful woman. Charming...and so young. You have so much life ahead of you."

Lovely, charming...and *young.* That final word destroyed the thoughts that had sent her flying. How could she tell Philip that age meant nothing to her? Lyle had been her age and she'd been miserable. Age had nothing to do with relationships. In Jemma's eyes, Philip was handsome, captivating…and young at heart. That's what counted.

She suppressed her frustration. "Philip, why do you insist on making yourself out to be Methuselah? You're only fifty."

He lowered his eyes and stared at his fingers clasped on the table in a tight knot. "I am fifty, Jemma…and I only meant that there's a wonderful world you've never experienced. I'm pleased to share a little of it with you."

A little of it? Jemma shifted her eyes toward the wide lake-view window, her focus drawn to the darkening horizon. She should be grateful to share a little, but at this moment, she would be grateful to share a lifetime with him.

Hearing Jemma's hesitant voice, Philip clenched the telephone to his ear. "What did you say?"

She cleared her throat. "I said that, uh—well, Claire wants me to ask if the job offer is still…"

Her voice faded, followed by a clatter of the receiver.

"Philip?" Claire's voice piped through the line.

"Yes, I'm here."

"She'll take forever at the rate she's going," Claire said, barreling through his response. "Jemma and I had a long talk this afternoon, and she's decided to take you up on your offer if you still have an opening at the resort."

"Sure, Claire," Philip said, discerning that Claire

had decided, not Jemma. "We can always use help." The distorted truth sailed from his mouth. At the moment, as far as Philip knew, he had a full staff—but Jemma wanted his help and he had to do something. "Claire, put Jemma back on."

He heard Claire's muffled instructions, and finally, Jemma's soft voice reached him. "I'm back, Philip."

"Listen, Jemma, right now it's probable that we only have an opening in Housekeeping, but I'm sure—"

"Don't apologize, please," she said. "Housekeeping is fine. I don't have skills for much of anything else anyway."

The ache in her voice cut through him, and he reined his rising emotion. "I'll call Personnel and tell them you're coming in. They'll be expecting you."

"Thank you," she said in a tentative voice. "I'll be there this afternoon."

When she disconnected, Philip fell back in his chair. Why hadn't she called a couple of weeks earlier? He could have offered her more options—a job she might have enjoyed and one that carried a higher salary.

Thinking, he tapped his fingers against the mahogany desktop. Maybe he could figure out a way to pay her a better salary…if he could keep it under wraps. No, too many people talked, and Jemma would be furious if she thought he'd given her preferential treatment.

He grabbed the telephone and punched in the Personnel extension. "Judy," he said when he heard her greeting, "a young woman will drop by this afternoon for a job. Jemma Dupre. She's a good friend…of the family. Is anything open besides Housekeeping?"

He listened to Judy tell him what he already knew.

"We have a full staff, Mr. Somerville, but we might have an opening in Laundry," Judy said.

Laundry? Sweltering, backbreaking work. Not Jemma. "Hire her for housekeeping, anyway, Judy. Someone will quit one of these days, and we'll have the extra help. Can you work something out?"

"Whatever you say. I'll shuffle the schedule."

Hearing her response, Philip ended the conversation and replaced the receiver. He could count on Judy to be subtle. Personnel was like that. She knew the employees' strengths and weaknesses, heard about their problems and sorrows. He could trust Judy to handle the situation.

But could he trust himself? Philip released a stream of air from his lungs. Since the day on the sailboat, his thoughts were filled with Jemma. He pictured her glowing face turned toward the sun, her golden hair tossed by the wind, her cheeks flushed with exhilaration.

Though she resented his comment, Jemma experienced life with a child's faith. Not immature, but innocent and expectant like a youngster at Christmas. Jemma touched his heart.

But the thought made him stop cold. She had so

much life to live, and he had so little to offer her. Between his responsibilities at the resort and his advanced age, he felt like a doddering grandfather fantasizing over a movie starlet. If Jemma was going to be underfoot day in and day out, Philip had to find a way to control his growing emotions. He needed God's help.

Jemma parked her new used car in the staff lot and strode into the resort. Though she'd accepted Philip's offer halfheartedly, each day she grew to love her work more. The staff was friendly, and the job paid very well compared to the job she'd had back in Monroe.

Giving a wave to one of her co-workers, Jemma headed for Housekeeping. Each day, she watched for Philip and though she saw him occasionally, he seemed to be only a fleeting image. He'd give her a quick wave and head in his own direction. But what did she expect?

He owned the resort. She cleaned the rooms.

Still, polishing the attractive furniture and burying her nose in the sweet-smelling percale sheets gave her pleasure. She'd lived with threadbare linens for too long not to appreciate quality bedclothes and thick towels.

"Jemma?"

Jemma turned and recognized her supervisor's pleasant sienna-toned face. "Good morning."

Latrice beckoned her into the linen room. "Carrie

said you wanted to talk with me.'' She shifted closer and lowered her voice. ''I hope nothin's wrong.''

Jemma shook her head. ''No, not at all. I just had some ideas and wondered if you'd be willing to hear them.''

Latrice tilted her head, eyeing her. ''Ideas? What do you mean?''

Though she'd been filled with confidence when she reviewed her proposals, Jemma now became strangely nervous. Would Latrice think she was too forward, wanting to change the world after only two weeks on the job?

''I've been talking to a few people who've worked at other resorts and—''

Latrice frowned. ''They're not happy here?''

''No, that's not it. I've asked about some of the other resorts' conveniences—things that appeal to customers.''

Though Latrice looked straight into her eyes, Jemma sensed the woman was puzzled.

''Well…I was thinking that this area has so many resorts, but what could make Bay Breeze different…and so I…'' She studied Latrice's puzzled expression. ''Should I go on?''

''You better, girl, 'cause I have no idea where you're headed.'' She loosed a piping chuckle.

''I'm talking about amenities,'' Jemma said. ''You know, special things that are added to the room. Things people talk about when they leave. It's good public relations and good advertising copy.''

"Like those big ol' terry-cloth robes," Latrice said. "Our suites have those."

"Yes, but I was thinking about something less expensive," Jemma said.

"Chocolates on the pillows?"

"Sure, that would be nice—but how about fresh flowers in each room, hot chocolate and tea to go along with the in-room coffeemakers?" Jemma watched a grin creep to Latrice's face.

"Girlfriend, you have some pretty fancy ideas."

"Maybe, but this is a pretty fancy resort, isn't it?" Jemma countered.

"You have me there," Latrice said, slapping her leg. "Let me talk to someone in Rooms Division. They'd be the first ones to listen to new ideas."

"Thanks," Jemma said. She took a step backward, wondering if Latrice was finished. "Then, I'd better get to work."

"You can say that again."

She handed Jemma a list of vacated rooms to be cleaned, and Jemma headed for the housekeeping supplies room on the second floor. She wasn't assigned the elegant suites, just nice rooms with balconies and king-size beds. Decorated in mauve and green, they reminded her of fresh spring flowers.

She bounced as she walked toward the elevator, knowing that her life had taken a positive turn. Ask and you shall receive. She hadn't thought God had time for her small problems. But she sensed her good fortune was a blessing, and today she felt spurred to send the Lord a thank-you.

Although she'd moved back with Claire for the present, her new older-model car gave her independence. In a few weeks the next big step would be finding an apartment.

And somehow she'd been inspired with these creative ideas. Today, telling them to Latrice had a second purpose. Jemma needed to prove herself. Philip had shown his usual charity by giving her a job at Bay Breeze. In fact, looking around at the number of housekeepers coming and going, Jemma even wondered if they were overstaffed.

No matter. Philip had given her a chance, and she wanted to prove her worth. If she could find new ways to make the resort even better, it would benefit Philip, prove her resourcefulness and offer him a kindness in return.

When she reached Housekeeping, Jemma put her shoulder bag in a locker and loaded the supply cart. Though she tried to concentrate on her tasks, her mind inevitably returned to sailing across the rolling blue water, watching Philip's capable hands at the helm.

Jemma didn't know why she'd become so fixated on Philip, but lately, she wished she were free of the growing desire that addled her mind. She'd experienced a marriage with a man tied to his work and personal interests while she longed for a happy home and family. She'd never wanted wealth. Jemma

would have been content to live with frayed uphol-
stery and nicked tables as long as she had a man by
her side who loved her and cherished her company.
Lyle hadn't been that man.

So why did she let Philip affect her so? His life-
style alone should deter her feelings. Like Lyle, he
spent long hours at the resort, burdened with the responsibilities of the vast complex of buildings and
grounds. He held the reins alone. She sometimes
sensed he preferred to be alone.

And worse, he considered her a child—a lovely,
charming, innocent child.

Would he ever recognize that she was a woman?
A woman who could love him if he would only let
her.

When Philip heard the tap on his office door, he
lifted his head.

Ian rested against the doorjamb, watching him.
"Do you have a minute?"

Philip beckoned him in. "Sure, sit down." He
moved the stack of letters to the side and rested his
back against the chair. "What's up?"

"Bob Campbell from Rooms Division mentioned
something about a new employee with some interesting ideas." He slid into a chair across from Philip.
"I guess Latrice told him. I didn't want to proceed
without asking your opinion."

"Interesting ideas? What, for example?"

"I'm not sure. Bob said room amenities. He

thought she had some good concepts." He shrugged. "He didn't go into detail."

Philip folded his hands across his belly and stretched his legs under his desk. "Room amenities, huh? Sounds like a budget consideration." He dragged a fading list from his memory bank. Terry robes, coffeemakers, ironing boards, hair dryers. What other amenities did they need? "Who is she?"

"The new housekeeper, you mean?" Ian asked.

Philip's chest tightened. Could he be referring to Jemma? "Right, the woman with the ideas."

He settled his glasses more firmly on his nose. "Jenna somebody, I think."

"Jemma," Philip corrected. "She's my cousin's daughter-in-law." He straightened his back. "She and my cousin had dinner with me here a while ago. You might remember." Philip remembered—the night of Andrew's surprising telephone call.

"Not really," Ian said with a shrug. But in an eye-blink, a knowing expression settled on his face. "Wait a minute. Is she blond? Really pretty?"

Philip nodded. Anyone who saw Jemma would remember her wispy, almost intangible, loveliness. Like a rare butterfly.

"Yes, I remember now. I was curious who she was. She sat beside you the night I interrupted you so often." He swung his arm in the direction of the hotel lobby. "I thought I saw her here the other day."

"That's her. Jemma Dupre. She moved to Loving

a while back with my cousin who's a widow. The one who opened that boutique over on Washington. Jemma lost her husband, too."

"She's single, then," Ian said. "Maybe it's time for you to find someone and settle down again, Philip. Good for you."

Philip tensed. "Good for me? Good for *nothing*. I'm old enough to be her father."

As he made the statement, Ian's younger age sent envy rising up Philip's back. Philip felt like a has-been king of the jungle, no longer able to compete with the forceful new males who stalked into the pride to lay claim to the lionesses. Philip had long passed that stage. And Jemma was a free woman. A woman who needed a virile young man—like Ian.

Looking puzzled, Ian rose. "Would you like me to talk with her, then?"

"Why not," Philip said, longing to talk with her himself. But he'd been doing his best to stay away. "Let me know if she suggests anything worth looking into."

"Sure thing." Ian turned and strode from the room.

Philip unknotted his fingers and rested his face in his hands. No matter what he said or how hard he pushed, Jemma haunted his thoughts. Obviously he had to take action or he'd be lost. Since meeting Jemma, Philip had realized he needed a woman, and Jemma needed a man to give her all the love she deserved. But they weren't right for each other.

He couldn't let himself fall in love. It wasn't fair to Jemma. She needed companionship and children, and Philip couldn't offer her either one. He was too busy to be good company and too old to be a father.

A man like Ian Barry was what she needed. Single. Good job. Money. Dependable. The thought stuck him like an ice pick, and a cold ache shivered through him.

"Oh, Jemma," he murmured. "Why can't you stay out of my thoughts?" His real fear pressed against his chest. Why couldn't she stay out of his heart.

Jemma fluffed the pillows she'd covered with fresh pillowcases, placed them back on the bed and covered both with the bedspread. After gathering the soiled linen, she stepped into the hall and disposed of it all at the cart. Then she returned to the room and switched on the vacuum cleaner.

With the roar of the machine in her ears, Jemma didn't hear the man enter. She jumped when a hand tapped her shoulder, and she swung around to face Ian Barry. Lifting her toe, she tapped the off button. The vacuum cleaner's drone died to silence.

"Sorry," he said. "I frightened you."

"That's okay. I didn't hear you with that thing roaring." She scanned his face, wondering if she'd done something to displease him or if possibly he'd returned to ask more about her suggestions.

A week earlier when he called her into his office,

she'd given him a brief rundown of ideas. But instead of being pleased at his interest, she'd felt disappointed that Philip hadn't asked to see her. He'd sent his assistant to speak with her. Now she was sure that Philip was avoiding her.

She focused on Ian. "Can I do something for you?" Waiting for his response, she tried to calm her anxiety.

"Yes," he said, adjusting his eyeglass frames. "Mr. Somerville would like to see you before you leave today."

"Mr. Somerville?"

"Philip," he said. "In his office."

"Did I—"

"It's about your ideas…the things we talked about last week."

From his response, Jemma realized her expression had shown concern. Her telling face was always like an open book.

"All right. Should I see him now…or after work?" Her pulse sprinted with her longing to run to him.

"Finish your rooms first," Ian answered.

She gave him a bright smile, praying her expression didn't show her disappointment. "Okay."

When she finished the vacuuming, she shoved the cart along the hall, flying from room to room in anticipation of her meeting. Her thoughts flew as quickly as her hands.

But Jemma's desires were a paradox. She wanted

her freedom, yet she longed for love. She wanted Philip, but she didn't want his help. She would only marry a Christian, but she wouldn't let the Lord guide her.

Why hadn't she given her troubles to God? Jesus stood with wide open arms, waiting for her to lay her burdens down. Instead, she swung from one emotion to the other, never understanding what she wanted, never listening to God's direction.

And what about Philip? When she'd finally asked about his faith, his answer had seemed evasive.

With her mind preoccupied, Jemma completed her day's work. She returned to the housekeeping storage room, stowed the cart and pulled her shoulder bag from the locker.

Looking into a small mirror, Jemma ran a comb through her unruly curls, then pulled them back with a clasp. She ran a pale-orange gloss on her lips, then slipped off her Bay Breeze smock and smoothed her knit top. When she finished, she drew in a lengthy breath. Courage was what she needed.

Waiting by the bank of elevators, Jemma tried to imagine what Philip would say to her. Would he apologize for his absence? Would he say he had missed her? The *ding* of the arriving car scattered her thoughts and she chided herself for her foolishness.

At the first floor, Jemma darted from the elevator, then held her eager steps to a brisk pace as she followed the hallway to the executive offices. The secretary wasn't at her desk, but Philip's door sat open. She peeked inside.

With his forehead braced in his hand, Philip bent over his work, a manila folder spread open in front of him. Jemma inched forward, but before she could tap, Philip lifted his head and noticed her. He rose.

"Come in, Jemma."

"You asked to see me," she said, willing her frazzled nerves to calm.

"Yes, I did." He gestured toward the easy chairs away from his desk. "Sit there. It's more comfortable."

She followed his direction and walked to the sitting area, pausing long enough to admire the lush brocade chair covering before sinking into its deep cushion.

Philip had not followed, but moved to a sideboard and pulled cups from a storage area. "Coffee?"

She nodded. "With a little cream, please."

He didn't look her way as he filled the cups. She waited, feeling like a stranger attending a business meeting. What had happened to the warm friendship that they'd shared? It's absence darkened her hopefulness.

Avoiding Philip's scrutiny, Jemma stared at the rug—an oriental one in the deepest shades of blue and red—rich and elegant...unlike Jemma, who today felt plain and poor in Philip's presence.

Philip's shadow fell across her arm, and she forced her eyes upward. He extended the coffee cup, which sent up an aroma of rich creamy hazelnut. She held the saucer against her lap and waited for him to sit.

He did, and when he looked at her he gave her a puzzled frown. "Is something wrong? I hoped that you'd like your work here."

"No, my job's fine."

"I'm glad." He lifted his cup and took a sip, eyeing her over the rim. When he lowered it, he kept his gaze riveted to her. "You look so concerned, Jemma. I asked you to see me because I've heard that you have some rather innovative ideas. I wanted to discuss them with you."

"Mr. Barry told me."

"Right."

His eyes glazed over, and she sensed he had drifted away from her, had dropped a barricade between them.

Two could play the game—if that's what he was doing. If he wanted to be distant and talk business, she could be as businesslike as anyone. She lifted her cup and sipped the hot brew, letting the flavor play on her tongue before swallowing.

Silence.

As if he had returned from his imaginary journey, he refocused on her. "Why not tell me about your ideas?"

Stiffening her resolve, she reviewed the same concepts she'd told Ian Barry, telling him how she'd gathered information from co-workers and pointing out the difference between everyday amenities and something unique.

"Chocolates on the pillow are commonplace, but hot chocolate and tea in the room aren't."

"You're right."

She could see his mind sorting and resorting her ideas. Struck by a new idea, she added, "Coffee mugs with the Bay Breeze logo would make a nice souvenir...with a minimal price tag."

"You have more ideas than I can comprehend, Jemma." He sent her the familiar smile that melted her heart. "I'll tell you what. Let me think about all you've said, and we'll meet again in a few days. I'll have a chance to hash out some details. How's that?"

"That's fine, but don't think you have to say they're good ideas just to make me happy."

"You don't need me to make you happy. I'm sure happiness finds you."

An odd look skidded across his face. She couldn't believe the man was that dense. If he didn't realize that he made her happier than anything on earth, Jemma decided, Philip Somerville must be a fool.

Chapter Six

Jemma leaped from her car and raced through the parking lot to the boutique door with her news. She hadn't been able to keep the smile off her face since she'd heard.

When she opened the door, the bell jingled, catching Claire's attention. Jemma sent her an excited grin.

"Jemma," Claire called from the counter. "Something's happened. I can see that telltale glow."

Laughter rumbled from Claire's chest, and her customer, Sissy Hartmann, gave Jemma a cheery wave as she hurried through the shop to join them.

"Do you have good news?" Sissy asked in her familiar confidential tone, leaning toward Jemma.

"I do." Jemma pressed her palms together and closed her eyes. Was it really true? She released a sigh, acknowledging that God had blessed her again. "I got a promotion."

"Promotion." Both women repeated the word and gasped at the same time.

Claire darted around the display counter and drew Jemma into a generous bear hug.

"Tell us," Sissy said, waiting with wide eyes.

When Claire released her, Jemma drew back and sputtered the rest of her story. "Philip called me into his office and said that my ideas were so impressive he was offering me the position of Specialties Director. It's part of Rooms Division."

"Oh my." Sissy's face drooped with concern.

"What?" Claire snapped. "It's a promotion."

"But what happened to the other director—?"

"He left the resort," Jemma said. "Don't worry Sissy, he wasn't fired."

Claire's expression changed to one of seeming relief.

Jemma rested her hand on Sissy's shoulder. "Philip said they were just ready to post the opening. And…" She waited for their full attention. "I'll get a raise."

"Oh, that's so nice," Sissy said, reaching to her shoulder where Jemma's hand rested and patting it. "I'm happy for you, my dear.

Jemma dropped her hand noting the petite woman seemed as nervous as a bird. "I'm just so excited."

"And you should be," Sissy said.

Claire lifted her hands in proclamation. "We should celebrate."

Jemma grinned and twirled in a full circle, stopping to face her mother-in-law. "And we are, Claire. Tonight Philip's taking us to dinner."

"Dinner. Fantastic," Claire said. "I hope I have something to wear."

Hearing Claire's concern, Jemma controlled a laugh. She couldn't think of a single time when Claire didn't have something unique to wear.

"Philip Somerville is a gem," Sissy said with a wispy, romantic sigh. "You're so blessed."

"I am." Jemma grinned, knowing she truly was.

Sissy shifted her attention to a leather purse, and Claire retraced her steps behind the counter. From the snatches of conversation, Jemma speculated the purchase would be a gift for Abby Hartman's birthday.

Wandering away from the handbag decision, Jemma stopped at the scarf table and organized the colorful silk accessories, placing them in neat rows. Her thoughts drifted back to her meeting that afternoon with Philip, when she'd first seen the delighted expression on his face. She'd had no doubt that the news he was about to tell her was extraordinary.

The promotion was a dream come true, but what stood out in Jemma's mind was how wonderfully natural Philip had been when he spoke to her that afternoon. Not businesslike as he'd acted during previous meetings, but the way he behaved at dinner or on the boat—like a friend. She prayed he would always treat her that way.

Whenever she sensed Philip shrinking away as he'd done recently, Jemma felt an ache deep in her chest. An emptiness as if someone had ripped out her heart. She pushed the awful thought away.

The shop bell tinkled, and Jemma turned toward the sound, surprised to see one of her co-workers enter the shop.

"Carrie." Jemma waved and left the scarves to greet her. "What are you doing here?"

"I've listened to you talk about the shop so often, I thought I'd stop by and take a look for myself," she said with a smile. "Besides, I need a birthday gift for my sister-in-law."

After getting a better idea what Carrie was looking for, Jemma guided her toward the items. At a leather goods display, Carrie examined the features of a clutch bag. When she was satisfied, she shifted her attention to Jemma. "So tell me about your meeting with Mr. Somerville. Is he really considering your ideas?"

Jemma nodded, unable to cover her glee. "He is—and guess what."

The woman shrugged.

"I'm so excited. He's made me the new Specialties Director."

A puzzled look settled on Carrie's face. "What's that?"

Jemma shrugged. "It's part of Rooms Division."

Carrie's expression gave Jemma a distressed feeling. "I'll put the new ideas into practice and make Bay Breeze a resort that people won't forget."

"You sound like a commercial." Carrie deepened her voice and mimicked a televison announcer. "Visit Bay Breeze, a resort you won't forget."

Laughing with her, Jemma clapped her hands. "That could be the new motto."

The questioning look returned to Carrie's face. "But I think this must be a new position, Jemma. I've been at Bay Breeze a long time and never heard of a Specialties Director…except for setting up conferences and banquets, maybe. I'm thinking it's part of the Food and Beverage Department."

Jemma shook her head. "No, Phi—Mr. Somerville said Rooms Division."

Carrie shrugged. "Oh well, it doesn't matter. You got a promotion. I'm so happy for you."

Jemma rang up the clutch bag, but after Carrie paid for her purchase and departed, Jemma felt unsettled. She sensed her friend was jealous of the promotion, and Jemma didn't like the way that made *her* feel. Would others react as Carrie had and think that Jemma had received special treatment? Most of her co-workers had no idea she and Philip knew each other. She'd been very careful about that.

Was it possible Carrie knew? Her reaction had the definite ring of jealousy.

Philip held the door for Claire and Jemma as they exited the Porte Bello Restaurant on the first floor of

Harborfront Place. He'd wanted to kick himself—erase the moment he'd made the offer to celebrate. What kind of a fool was he? Recently, he'd begun concocting a scheme to push Jemma and Ian together, hoping they'd fall in love—but at the same time, he was setting himself up for grief. And when Jemma glowed after he told her about the position, and he couldn't hold back his own excitement.

"That was a treat," Claire said. "The food was delicious, and my new dentures feel wonderful." Stepping from the air-conditioning into the warmer outside air, she pulled the purple shawl from her shoulders.

"I'm glad you took care of that," Philip said, pleased that he'd cautioned Bill Barrow to give her a low price.

Philip was also pleased that Claire had worn one of her more subdued outfits that evening—an ankle-length, purple print dress. The most outlandish part of her costume was a large silk orchid she'd pinned behind her ear.

Jemma paused on the walk, looking toward the Grand River across the street. "What's that grandstand for?" She pointed to the weathered structure on the waterfront.

"Musical Fountain," Philip said. "The show doesn't begin until after dark."

She turned toward him, a scowl wrinkling her forehead. "Musical fountain? What's it do?"

As he'd done so often, Philip ignored his common sense and looked at his wristwatch. "Would you like to stick around and see?"

"I'd love to, if it's all right with everyone." She shifted her focus to Claire.

Her mother-in-law gave a deep yawn. "It'll be nearly ten before it starts, don't you think, Philip?"

"Probably," he agreed. "Is that too late, Claire?"

She gave him a one-shoulder shrug. "The shop opens early. Would it be too much trouble to give me a ride home first?"

He knew he should offer a rain check, but he'd already muzzled his good sense. "Not at all, Claire if you're sure."

"No, please." Jemma held up her hand, waving away his words. "Don't go through all that trouble for me. Some other time would be fine."

"No, you two enjoy yourselves," Claire said.

With Claire helping the decision, Philip led them back to the car and headed toward Loving, calculating that he had plenty of time to return before show time.

When they pulled in behind the boutique, Jemma again protested going back, but Claire stifled her argument. After saying good-night to Claire, Philip watched her safely into the apartment, then drove the few miles back to the waterfront stands.

A small crowd had gathered on the boardwalk, while others had selected seats in the bleachers. Philip noticed some had jackets and a few carried car blankets. Since the sun had set, a cooler breeze drifted off the river, and he eyed Jemma's short sleeves.

"Will you be too cold?"

"No, it's pleasant." She turned to him, her face stressed. "But I still feel badly that you came all the way back here just for me."

"I haven't seen the fountain show in years, and I'll enjoy it as much as you." He supported her elbow as she took the steps into the bleachers and settled on a plank seat.

Alerted by a cool breeze that fluttered across his back, Philip again eyed Jemma's bare arms. "Wait here, and I'll run back and—"

"I'm not a child, Philip." She shook her head, teasing him and yet making a point. "It's summer. I won't freeze."

Her playful smile sparked a trail of warmth to his belly. Philip closed his mouth. Why press the issue? Jemma was not a child. She was pure woman. That was his problem.

Thinking back, Philip remembered his first meeting with Jemma. He'd enjoyed her inexperience and freshness. At the time, he'd thought she was like a child. But he'd been totally wrong. Now he was suffering the consequences of giving his emotions free rein. He had to be more watchful.

At dinner that evening, Philip had let down his guard and unsettled himself by the thoughts that lingered in his mind—no matter how much he fought them. Now, he pictured her at Porte Bello, poring over the menu, wisps of her upswept hair trailing on her neck. He had yearned to run his fingers through her natural curls, to hold her in his arms and feel her lips against his.

Gooseflesh rose on his arms. How long had it been since he'd kissed a woman? How would her mouth feel pressed against his? Would Jemma part her lips for him while he reveled in the pliant softness of her mouth?

After dinner when she sneaked her lipstick from her bag and subtly drew it across her lips, he'd been captivated, unable to look away. Even the remembrance produced a longing deep inside him.

As a cold gust flapped the hem of Philip's suit jacket, lights rose along the river's distant bank and a solitary geyser shot into the air. The water spray ascended as a bright-red glow, and a voice pierced the darkness, announcing the start of the performance.

While the fountain-voice offered statistics to the viewing audience, another puff of wind passed them, and Jemma shivered. Without asking, Philip tugged his arm from his jacket, slid it off the other, and wrapped it over Jemma's shoulders.

She sent him a frown. "No, Philip."

"I'm not going to let you freeze."

She swung the jacket from her shoulders and held it on one finger. "Put this back on or I'll drop it."

He'd never met such a stubborn woman. He eyed

the darkness below the bleacher seats and nabbed his coat before she let it fall. He slipped his arm into one side and tried to put the other shoulder around her for warmth.

"Put your jacket on," she demanded.

Her voice triggered his own determination. "All right, but let me put my arm around you, then."

She didn't argue about that, and when he'd donned the coat, he nestled her against him and covered her arm with his. He felt her burrow into his side, and a part of him was pleased that she'd insisted on remaining coatless.

Music filled the air, and with the rise and fall of the melody, the water sprays dipped and swirled washed in varied colors. Jemma oohed and aahed at the display, vocalizing appreciative utterances in the night.

Jemma's sweet scent swept passed him on the breeze, and Philip buried his cheek in her hair and drew in the intoxicating aroma. For once, Jemma didn't inch away, but seemed happy in his arms.

Philip allowed his hand to explore the satiny texture of her skin, the soft down of her arm prickling upward with the cooler air. Garnering courage, he rested his palm over her hand and wrapped her chilled fingers in his. His reward was Jemma's delicate squeeze, seeming to let him know his boldness was approved.

How much would this cold night unloose their restraints? A love song filled the night sky, accompanied by the muted greens and blues of the water's spray, and Jemma's body pulsed to the music's rhythm. As the passion of the melody swelled, the hues danced on the water like red and orange flames.

As the song faded, Jemma tilted her head upward, and Philip was lost in her shadowed gaze. He slid his hand up the silk of her arm and lifted her chin. He longed to kiss her, but drew away.

Jemma's surprised, expectant eyes caught his, and he felt like a high school boy sitting on the bleachers, trying to sneak his first kiss.

He opened his mouth to apologize, to tell her he would never try to kiss her again, but he swallowed the words. He would not say he was sorry. No promises. In his heart, he knew apologies and promises might someday be broken.

Disappointment swirled in Jemma's mind. Confused, she directed her eyes to the fountain for the finale. After the last melody ended, they made their way down the bleacher stairs.

Philip had withdrawn as he so often did. When they reached the car, he opened the door for her, then headed for the driver's side and climbed in. She sensed he wanted to speak, but only his eyes seemed to reflect the words her heart longed to hear.

Why had he drawn back? He'd been so sweet and caring. She'd been positive that he'd wanted to kiss her. Her own heart yearned to have his lips against hers. But something had stopped him.

Now in the driver's seat, Philip kept his hands on

the wheel, his eyes focused on the highway. In the quiet, Jemma relived the gentle touch of his hands and the longing look in his eyes. She realized how long it had been since she'd felt such emotion.

When she dug into her vague memories, regret evaded her. Lyle had never stirred her heart as it had been stirred tonight. His passion had been selfish and fleeting. Though she had always honored her duty as a wife, she'd felt unfulfilled.

Tonight in Philip's company, she had felt like a woman—loved and needed. But now that he'd nearly kissed her, things would be different. How could she see him at Bay Breeze and not remember that moment when she'd been cooled by the wind yet warmed by desire?

She studied his profile, silhouetted by the passing streetlights—his eyes staring straight ahead, his jaw tense. What would happen now?

Instead of feeling hope, Jemma was washed by despair. *Dear Lord, please don't let this dream of happiness become a nightmare.*

Chapter Seven

Jemma hadn't slept well. Every few minutes during the night, she had stared at the illuminated clock hands and wondered where her life was headed.

Caught up in the romantic moment, she'd allowed her good sense to vanish. No matter how kind and tender Philip was when they were together, it changed nothing. He was a workaholic, and, for all she knew, a non-believer.

She thought back over their conversations and tried to recall if he'd ever spoken about God's saving grace. Her question sat uneasily in her mind. Had she ever talked with Philip about her own faith? If having a relationship with the Lord was truly important to her, she'd not been a good example. Her faith was hanging by a weak thread most of the time.

Still, she wanted to know. How could she announce that she was unwilling to form a lasting relationship with a man who didn't live according to God's rules? She'd sound like a fool. Philip had never claimed he wanted anything more than a friendship.

Jemma knew from experience that she wanted a Christian husband. Shame lodged in her heart when she thought about Lyle's wasted money and misguided adventures. He'd lead others astray with his advice and take their money for ill-conceived investments. And Jemma had been aware of it, but hadn't known what to do. How could she turn her back on her husband, when God's law opposed divorce?

The church said that marriage was for better or worse—and yet, what did a woman do when the *worse* went against God? She'd been caught in the middle. How could a wife win in that situation? Still, she should have spoken out and warned Lyle's unsuspecting friends of his recklessness.

After tossing throughout the night, Jemma woke with heavy eyes and swung her legs over the edge of her small bed in Claire's apartment. Rather than worry about things that didn't affect her—things from her past and hopeless dreams of the future—she had to take action. She wanted her own place, and she needed to unleash herself from Philip. Somehow, along the way, she'd forgotten her goal.

Independence.

Slipping on her robe, Jemma made her way to the kitchen and started the coffeemaker, then dumped cereal into a bowl. After filling her cup, she sank into the chair and faced her breakfast.

Noise came from the hall, and Claire came through the doorway. "I'm following my nose," she said, heading straight for the liquid energy. She poured a cup and sank into a chair.

"Not feeling well?" Claire asked, looking concerned. "I hope you're not catching a cold. I imagine it cooled off last night and you didn't have a coat."

"I was fine." With Philip's arms around her. "I'm just a little tired. I didn't sleep well."

"That's too bad. Did you enjoy the fountain? I haven't seen it in years, but I can remember how pretty it is."

"It was lovely."

"Good," Claire said. "Then, you had a nice time."

Jemma lifted the cup and took a slow, thoughtful sip. She had had more than a nice time. It had been wonderful...until reality set in.

"Philip's a good man, Jemma. He's a little older than you, but he has a lot to offer a woman. You should give that some—"

"Claire, don't plan my life, please." Jemma slammed her cup onto the table, and coffee sloshed over the edge. "Look, I'm sorry, but—"

"It's okay," Claire said with hurt in her eyes. She bit her lip and looked at the splotch of coffee.

Filled with remorse, Jemma wadded her paper napkin and daubed at the spill. Claire was good to her, and all she'd done was cause Claire extra work and worry.

"You don't need me adding stress to your life," Jemma said, patting Claire's tensed hand. "I need to look for my own place one of these days. Instead of worrying about me, you should be taking care of yourself. What about a man for you?"

"Me?" Claire's eyebrows arched above her widened eyes. "I've been alone for years...and like it. But you're young, Jemma. You should have children and a husband who'll take care of you."

"I can take care of myself." Her voice rang with confidence—but could she? She'd muddled things too often.

"I know you *can,* but wouldn't it be lovely to find someone who could take care of you?"

Jemma understood what she meant, but she didn't agree. Yet she saw no sense in disagreeing with Claire. "If I ever fall in love again, I want a man who loves the Lord as much as he loves me."

Claire's mouth opened and closed like a fish out of water. Jemma figured that perhaps for the first time in Claire's life she'd been rendered speechless.

"Lyle went to church once in a while," Jemma continued, "but he didn't know the Lord. Not really. This time I want a man who's walking the same path I'm walking." She shook her head. "The same path I'm *trying* to walk. I know I'm a failure, but at least I know what God expects...and I feel remorse when I break the commandments."

Claire's face sagged with her own grief. "I know, Jemma. You didn't have a chance with Lyle. He was too much like his father."

Rising, Claire brought the coffeepot to the table and filled their nearly empty cups. Finished, she returned the pot to the counter, her words tumbling out. "Philip went to church years ago, I recall. His mother was a good Christian woman. Maybe some rubbed off."

Jemma didn't comment, and when Claire returned to the table, Jemma explained her concern. "I don't think Philip goes to church, and he's never talked about his faith to me."

"Men don't much. They probably think it's weak to lean on anyone. Even the Lord. But I'd guess he knows Jesus more deeply than you suspect."

"Maybe," Jemma said, wondering if Claire was right. And if she faced the truth, how much did Jemma lean on her own faith? She needed to get back to church more regularly…to lean on God for guidance. Heaven knows she didn't have the answers. Not a one.

Philip parked behind the boutique and sat for a moment. He'd come so close to alienating Jemma. That was the last thing he wanted to do. He cared for her…loved her. If he were a younger man, he'd offer her his love and every good thing that he could. But it was impossible.

He'd learned an important lesson in his marriage

to Susan. She'd expected so much of him, and Philip had been unable to be the husband she wanted. He had watched her spirit sag as illness took over. By then it was too late to change. Too late to make up for the hours of loneliness and longing she'd endured in silence.

Silence. A smile came to his lips, tugging him from his reverie. Jemma would never be silent. That's one thing no man would have to fear. She'd speak her mind whether a husband cared to hear it or not. She'd pull and push until she got what she wanted. Along with her innocent charm, Jemma had been given the gift of spirit…and determination. She was a fighter in her own modest way.

Philip pushed open the car door and swung his legs to the ground. The gravel crunched beneath his feet as he shoved the door closed and drew in a deep breath. Whether Jemma wanted his aid or not, he planned to help her in every way he could.

Yesterday, he'd gotten the lead on an apartment that he wanted her to see, and then he hoped to play cupid. Jemma and Ian. Jemma deserved a good man who could give her a good life. If Philip couldn't be that man, he'd see to it that he found her one. His annual Fourth of July party was an opportunity for him to play matchmaker. He prayed Ian and Jemma would hit it off. The prayer punctured his heart like a dagger. But that's how it had to be.

Philip entered the side door and, hearing voices, passed the workroom as he headed for the boutique.

When he stepped inside, Claire caught his eye with a wave. He looked around the shop, searching for Jemma. She wasn't there, but he spied Bodkin strutting toward him. He assumed Jemma was getting ready.

He wandered through the rows of displays, the cat at his heels, noticing the new merchandise—silk T-shirts, shawls and attractive knit sweaters. Claire's personal taste might be considered over the top, but her inventory had class.

With her bright smile and chatter, Claire moved from customer to customer with an eccentric cheeriness that mesmerized the patrons. Their conversation was punctuated by laughter and an animation that gave him a sense all was well with Claire's business.

"Philip," she said, waving a breezy goodbye to the last customer. "I hear you're taking Jemma out this evening."

Her arched eyebrow triggered his concern. He should set Claire straight, but his words would be repeated in Jemma's ear, so he could only agree. "Nothing special. I have something to show her." Seeing Claire's inquiring look, he added, "It's a surprise."

"Ah. But it's good to see you and Jemma together. She's a lovely woman, and a man like you has a lot to offer…if you know what I mean."

He'd be stupid if he didn't. He shook his head and chuckled. "Claire, subtlety is not your forte." And looking at her latest 1920s getup, his comment had a double meaning. He grinned at her dress covered in bright-red fringe and her tousled hair escaping from beneath a cloche hat.

At his comment, she gave her throaty laugh and swung out from behind the counter, nabbed Bodkin in her arms and sashayed to the new display. There she dropped her furry friend. She unfurled a white cashmere shawl, seeded with fresh-water pearls. "What do you think?"

"Very nice, Claire…and obviously expensive."

She gave him a knowing grin and refolded the cloth, just as the door tinkled and two women swept into the shop.

"I'd better find Jemma," Philip said, turning toward the doorway. But he faltered when Jemma stepped into the room. Dressed in blue and white, she looked so fresh and appealing. Confusion shivered through him.

"I'm ready," she said. "I already grabbed a bite to eat."

Her comment checked his plan to take her to dinner. Maybe he would stop for coffee later so they could talk. "I parked in back."

She turned toward the side door, and he followed.

Once on the road, he alerted Jemma that he needed to make a stop, without offering an explanation. She didn't ask. He followed the highway that led to the resort, but before reaching the sprawling complex he turned onto a residential street.

Jemma remained quiet. She kept her head turned away from him, looking out the passenger window. He suspected she was annoyed with his stop, but she didn't make a comment until he pulled in front of a two-story house.

"Where are we?" she asked.

"This is the stop I mentioned." He jumped out, rounded the car and opened her door.

She gave him a questioning look.

"Come with me. We're expected."

Her eyes narrowed, sending him the signal that she was irritated. He waited for the worst but was pleasantly surprised. Jemma slid from the car and followed him.

When the door opened, an elderly woman beamed a smile and pushed open the screen door for them to enter. Philip stepped into a narrow foyer with stairs leading to the second floor.

The woman pulled her door closed. "Here we go," the woman said, flagging Jemma to follow and climbing the stairs in front of them. "I'm Jeanette Luddy."

"Philip Somerville," he said, trying not to sound out of breath as he trudged up the stairs. At the top, he gestured. "This is Jemma Dupre. She's the one looking for a place."

Jemma only gave a slight nod.

"How do you do?" the woman said, selecting a key from a small ring. "Here, we go." She turned the key in the lock and pushed open the door, stepping aside to allow them entrance.

Jemma lingered in the hallway, her face tight with displeasure.

"Come. Come," the woman said, motioning her inside.

With her hands jammed into her sweater pockets, Jemma stepped into the room. When she was inside, her frown nailed Philip to the spot.

"Take your time," Jeanette said, "and when you're ready, just tap on my door." She grabbed the knob and pulled the door closed as she backed out of the room.

Jemma just stood there.

"I heard about this place and thought it would be perfect. It comes furnished," Philip said, breaking the uncomfortable silence. "I know you've been looking and—"

"And you had to help. You can't learn to let people make their own decisions, can you. I'm not your child, Philip. I have a brain. I can find my own place."

He stepped toward her, wanting to calm her, but her expression warned him off. He backed up a step. "I'm sorry, Jemma. I thought you might like the place."

"It has nothing to do with liking or disliking. It has to do with making my own decisions—solving my problems."

He ached for her and for himself. When would he

learn that Jemma didn't want his help. She hated it. "I know you can make your own decisions. I'm not trying—"

"You know?" Her voice reeked with sarcasm.

"I'm sorry. I made a mistake."

"A big mistake," she said.

He tucked his hands in his pants pockets to shackle the longing to take her in his arms. "Listen if you want to leave, we can. But we're here, so why not look at the place. It's close to work. You could walk if you wanted."

For the first time since they'd entered the flat, Jemma's face softened, and she focused on something other than him. She scanned the room—a large furnished sitting area and a small alcove with a table and four chairs.

She wandered across the room and entered the kitchen. He followed and stood at the door. The kitchen was small but useful. When she turned around, she brushed past him and headed for the opposite doorway. He didn't follow but leaned against the doorjamb and waited.

She took her time. He could hear her open the closet door, then the linen closet, then her heels tapping on bathroom floor tile. When she returned, she paused in the doorway. "It's very clean. Pretty wallpaper in the bedroom. I'm surprised."

He wanted to ask her why she was surprised, but he figured he'd done enough damage, so remained quiet. She reminded him of Andrew in a way. His brother didn't want anyone's help, either. He struck out on his own…and failed. But at least he'd had his independence. Jemma wouldn't fail. In that way, she was different.

Jemma headed toward him, and he stepped out of her way. She returned to the kitchen. This time, she looked through the cabinets, tested the stove, ran water in the sink and sniffed the refrigerator like a bloodhound.

Watching her detailed inspection, Philip kept his smile at bay. In his opinion, the place was perfect and the price was even better.

When she was finished, she stood for a moment in the center of the room, her eyes scanning the surroundings. Then she focused on him.

As he waited, his chest tightened.

"It's nice," she said.

He nodded.

"Do you know how much rent she wants?"

He nodded. "Four hundred a month."

Her eyes widened. "That's all?"

"That's all. No hidden costs, except your own telephone."

"Only a fool would pass this up."

That's what he'd thought, but he clamped his mouth shut.

"Thanks. You were thoughtful to bring me here."

"I was, wasn't I."

She gave a quiet chuckle. "I guess I can tap on Jeanette's door."

"Guess you can." She linked her arm in his, and he looked toward heaven with a humble thank-you.

Jemma slid the menu behind the metal napkin holder and shifted her gaze toward Philip. He meddled and he pushed. Sometimes he was impossible. And for once, she didn't care. Looking at him took her breath away. Though she'd tried not to fall in love, she'd finally admitted to herself that she had done just that. Now all she had to do was get Philip to love her in return.

She suspected he did. He just didn't know it yet.

Philip eyed her over the menu. "What are you having?"

"Death by Chocolate. I figure if I have to go, it might as well be a memorable experience."

His face broke into a bright smile. He'd been so tense all evening that Jemma felt guilty.

"I might go for the peanut butter pie. I can hear my arteries screaming as I speak."

Laughter cured many ills, and Jemma allowed herself to enjoy the moment. "Philip, I'm sorry I was so awful."

"Awful? Which time?"

An unexpected guffaw slipped from her throat. She gave his arm a playful smack and lowered her head, peeking around, praying that no one had heard her loud laugh. She would have given money for a photograph of his delightful expression.

"Now that we've resolved that," Philip said, "I'm glad you agreed to come with me."

"Me, too. It's been...interesting."

"And productive. By the way, if you need help moving, I'd be glad..." His voice faded as she glowered.

A waitress stepped to the table, took their order and moved away. Alone again, he shook his head as if defeated. "I'm sorry, I seem to step on your toes all the time."

"I understand. It's just you. You can't help the way you are."

"That sounds dire."

"It is at times. I don't know if we're friends or strangers."

Sadness washed over his face. "I'm sorry about that. Sometimes I don't know if I'm my own friend."

"When I'm with you, like we are right now, you make me laugh and I feel comfortable, but sometimes I'm confused. At the office, you're my employer so I don't know how to behave. I don't know if boss-employee friendships are allowed."

"We don't have rules regulating friendships at Bay Breeze. Loving is too small a village for that." He leaned forward and rested his elbow on the table. "Is something bothering you...at the resort?"

Jemma's chest tightened. Was this the time to tell him her concern? Carrie wasn't the only one who prodded her with an occasional question or gave her a curious glance. "I get looks from people some-times."

"Looks?" The tenderness vanished and he tensed.

"Questioning looks. It's probably just me. I worry that everyone assumes you gave me the job because I'm a friend. I wasn't here long enough for a pro-motion."

Philip knotted his fingers together. "Most people don't realize that you are a...friend, do they?"

"I've been discreet, Philip. I've told no one."

His jaw tightened and he narrowed his eyes. "Even if they know, it's not anyone's business but ours. You have the position because you deserve it. You're creative and dependable."

His angry defense startled her. "Thank you," she said, flustered by his compliments.

"From the beginning, I admired how hard you worked. Latrice always keeps me posted on new em-ployees. You deserved the promotion."

Jemma lowered her eyes, feeling foolish that she'd worried. Why did she assume people were talking about her? From the first day she took the job, every-one had been pleasant. Since her promotion, some asked about her education and acted surprised when she explained she'd never gone to college. But they'd been nothing but kind.

"Jemma."

Pulling herself back, she refocused on Philip. "Sorry, I was thinking."

"Thinking about how confusing I am?"

She shrugged. "Life's confusing, I guess. I just wonder what you're thinking. I wonder if I'm deluding myself and if you're just putting up with me for Claire's sake."

"Don't be foolish."

"But sometimes you're so distant, and I don't understand why. If it's my job, I'll find something else. I enjoyed our rela—friendship. I don't want to lose it."

Philip was stung by her words. He watched her eyes mist and longed to hold her in his arms, to brush the tears from her eyes. "Please don't cry."

He didn't know what to say. Glancing over his shoulder, Philip hoped customers hadn't noticed her tears—she would be embarrassed. He was miserable. How could he explain his feelings to her? What could he tell her other than that he wished he were fifteen years younger.

Jemma brushed her eyes with the back of her hand and straightened her back. "I don't expect you to take care of us anymore. Claire's doing well with the store. Since the tourists arrived, she's busy. I even have to help her sometimes in the evenings."

"I'm glad. Really."

"I just want us to be natural, Philip. Not like two strangers talking at a bus stop. Since I've moved to Loving, I haven't made a lot of friends, and the few I have are precious."

Precious! The word lit the sky. She'd compressed the reason for his struggle into that one word. She was the most precious thing in his life. From the day they'd met she'd dragged his emotions out of hiding. Her smile sent his pulse on a chase, made his limbs weak. But he stifled the sensation.

"I treasure your friendship, Jemma. I do." Philip struggled to keep himself from saying more.

She lifted her misted eyes, but before she could respond, the waitress arrived with their coffee and Jemma's Death by Chocolate, saving him from digging his own grave.

Chapter Eight

"What do you think?" Philip asked.

Ian shifted in the chair, apparently weighing the idea. "You're the boss. But..."

"But what?" Philip rose from his chair, came around his desk and propped a hip on its polished surface.

"I don't understand your strategy. It would help if I saw the need for all of this."

Philip understood his strategy but he couldn't explain it to Ian. "I think you should pick Jemma's brain. Maybe the two of you could scout out some of the other resorts and see what they're doing to draw in guests. That seems clear to me."

Ian frowned and stared at the floor. As if in thought, he propped an ankle across his knee and tugged at his navy-blue dress sock. "I know she has some interesting ideas...but we don't *need* to bring in more guests, do we?'' He lifted curious eyes to Philip's. "We have a full house most of the time.''

"Most of the time, yes. How about the winter months? We want to grow, Ian, not stand still...and that's what we're doing.''

Philip could see from Ian's expression that he didn't agree, but being a good employee he pushed his opinion aside.

"Like I said, you're the boss.'' Ian lifted his hand and, in his characteristic gesture, adjusted his eye-glass frames. "So then, what is it you want me to do?'' He leaned forward. "Don't get me wrong, Philip. I don't mind spending time with her. She's a good-looking woman.... That is—'' he looked pointedly at Philip "—if you're not interested.''

The words hit Philip like an arrow, and he reminded himself of his reason for continuing with his plan to make a match between Jemma and Ian. "Look at me.'' Philip touched his more-salt-than-pepper hair. "What would a young woman want with an old codger like me?''

"Codger? Don't be ridiculous You're in your prime. You need to get away from this place more often. Have you ever looked at the women around you? And their come-hither eyes? You're a good catch—nice-looking, respected and wealthy. What more could they want?''

Philip knew what more they wanted, and it wasn't a man like him. "Nice try, Ian.'' He swung back around his desk and sank into the chair. "Now, let's talk about the Fourth of July."

"The Fourth of July?"

"Right. I'm working out details now, and I've decided to have Jim Mason on as manager so you're free to help with my party upstairs. You and Jemma, that is."

Ian frowned. "Why Jemma?"

"Why not? I figured you could meet guests at the door. You know, help me out. That's why I have assistants."

With a look of resignation, Ian shrugged. "Sure if that's what you want. I'd rather spend the night looking at her face than my own."

Philip felt the same, but he wouldn't let it happen. "Okay, that's settled. Now, let's get back to visiting the resorts."

Ian opened his notepad, scribbling the instructions as Phillip reviewed what needed to be done. When he finished, Ian closed the folder, rose and headed toward the door. "Are you talking with Jemma about this or should I?"

A weight fell against Philip's chest. "You can go over things with her. I'm counting on both of you."

Ian gave him a thumbs-up, opened the door and exited, leaving Philip feeling very much alone.

Pivoting in his desk chair, Philip faced the dark water outside his window. What was he doing? Pushing two people together who he thought were good for each other. He was playing God and he knew it.

He closed his eyes, hearing Ian's words ricochet through his mind. *You're a good catch—handsome, respected and wealthy.* He eyed his vague reflection in the night-shrouded window. He wasn't confident about the good-looking part, but two out of three wasn't bad. Ian was correct. Philip guessed a few women out there didn't care about companionship and children as long as the man was respected and wealthy.

After Susan died, he'd pretty much dismissed romance from his life. First because of grief, and later, self-pity, and now… He shrugged. He should look for an older woman who'd raised her children and now wanted some of life's luxuries. Maybe he'd enjoy a woman's company.

Maybe? He chided himself. He'd enjoyed Jemma's companionship more than he could admit. Sailing, talking over dinner, laughing at anything. And longing to kiss her. He'd rethought that night a thousand times. The image showered him with pleasure and pain. His hand tingled with the memory of her silky skin and the affection in her eyes. But most often he was nailed by pain and guilt. He knew better than to tempt himself. He had to get his floundering emotions under control.

The time had come. He had to push himself to socialize again. Philip's mind trudged through the past years, older women he knew—women who made it clear more than once that they would enjoy spending time with him. If he spent time with a woman his age, perhaps Jemma would fade from his thoughts. His Fourth of July was an annual highlight of the summer. He'd ask someone to be his guest. But who? He had no idea.

He'd never ask Jemma. She deserved more. He didn't know much about her life with Lyle. But he knew Lyle. A smooth operator. He was like a sleight-of-hand artist. Now you see it, now you don't. Philip was sure Lyle had Jemma under his spell and married before she realized that it was all tricks.

How did Claire birth such a son? She was eccentric but a good woman. A Christian woman. Sluggish in her faith perhaps, but he could remember her speaking about her beliefs, and he knew she prayed. Lyle Senior had to be the flawed genetic factor. Not Claire.

Sadness filled him, thinking of sweet, innocent Jemma in a bad marriage with a man who tried to do magic with flawed props. He had failed. And Jemma? She was left with nothing. No husband, no children, no home—but a whole truckload of distrust and insecurity. And a tremendous drive to be free and independent. Philip couldn't blame her for wanting to stand on her own.

So why did he continue to manipulate her life? He rubbed the back of his neck, tensed by his own guilt. Because he had as strong a drive to make up for his past—to prove he could be generous, to prove he could take care of someone...and to prove he could care for someone—*love* someone—as much as he loved himself.

But who was he trying to convince? Himself or God?

Jemma hung her robe on the hook inside her closet and closed the door. She gazed around her cozy bedroom, at home for the first time in too long. Though she wished Philip would learn not to manipulate her life, she was pleased that he'd found the flat for her. A comfortable feeling warmed Jemma. Philip cared about her, no matter what he said.

In the mirror, she eyed her coordinated outfit and smoothed a wrinkle from her skirt, deciding she looked fine for church. She cringed as she wondered about Claire. When she had lived at the apartment, she had been able to suggest that Claire wear something less dramatic, but today, she asked the Lord to put a message in the woman's ear, suggesting a little decorum.

Jemma grinned, thinking about God wasting time worrying about Claire's wardrobe. She locked her door and hurried down the stairs. At the bottom, she glanced at Jeanette's closed door. The woman seemed the perfect landlady—quiet, yet there if Jemma needed her. Outside, Jemma slid inside her car and aimed the vehicle toward the boutique.

She loved Sunday mornings, and spending quality time with the Lord. And she often had Sunday off. Sometimes she wondered if that was a gift from

Philip just like so many things in her life seemed to be.

Today the streets were empty, the shops closed until noon and most people asleep—a relief during the busy summer season. Jemma smiled at the bright July sky, willing to admit that she needed to refocus on her goals and on the Lord.

She had begun to revitalize her faith. She'd grown tired of the more solemn church she'd attended when she first came to Loving. Certainly God's Word was preached there, but the congregation was as stiff as their suits and dresses, and as formal as their Sunday celebration.

A few weeks ago, she'd spotted a sign outside the Fellowship Church only a short distance away from the boutique. It read "If you can't find the spirit, look here." She had, and the sign had been correct. Powerful sermons, songs of praise and a friendly congregation. That's what she needed.

Her other issue was not as easy to solve. Her goal. While she struggled for independence, her heart kept leading her down a different path. A path that led to Philip. She needed to talk with the Lord on that one.

Before Jemma could toot the horn, Claire came through the side door of the shop, and Jemma released a thankful sigh. Claire wore a navy dress with matching pumps. The only color in her outfit was a multi-hued silk scarf fluttering behind her that she'd wrapped around her throat.

"Good morning," Claire said, yanking open the

passenger door. "Be honest. Do I look all right? Everything I wanted to wear needs cleaning." She tugged at the skirt of her dress. "I had to drag out this old rag. I think I wore it once to a funeral."

A chuckle sputtered from Jemma's chest. "I'm not laughing at you. When you walked through the door, I thought how nice you looked."

"I'll chalk your comment up to tact," Claire said, patting Jemma's knee.

Claire chattered as Jemma drove the short way to church. Inside, pre-service music filled the air, and Jemma guided them to seats somewhere in the middle. She glanced through the newsy program, reading the special announcements and long list of scheduled activities. Her attention was drawn to the choir's summer concert, a nice event to draw in the tourists. If Jemma had more time, she'd enjoy singing with the choir.

When the service began, the air hummed with praise and joy. If a weak Christian couldn't sense the Lord in this place, he was hopeless. Jemma thought of Philip. Was that his problem? Maybe he'd been lulled to sleep by his conservative faith and needed a little shot of the Holy Spirit.

Jemma wished she could tell Claire her real feelings. But the older woman had a way of meddling that made Jemma clench her teeth in frustration.

Shifting closer to Claire, she pointed to the notice. "I was thinking we might enjoy this concert."

Claire scanned the paragraph. "Sounds good to

me,'' Claire whispered, "if I could get the shop door closed on time. I could use a little midweek uplifting.''

Jemma steadied herself. "So could Philip. He's too tied to that resort.''

"That man does work too hard. He needs to relax. I ought to give him a call.''

Jemma was relieved. She should have known she could count on Claire...and the Heavenly Father. She lifted her gaze to the stained-glass window—a cross between the descending dove and the eye of God.

Jemma stood near Ian at Philip's front entrance, awed by the lovely setting and the guests who swarmed into the penthouse apartment. She'd never been in Philip's rooms before, though she'd seen the elevator marked Private that took him to his own quarters in the resort.

Sometimes she wondered why he'd never shown her his quarters, but then she answered her own question. Philip was very private and protective of their relationship.

Protective? Or embarrassed?

In Philip's company, Jemma often forgot that she was the "poor relation.'' She forgot she lacked education and social polish. God had given her creative ideas and a flair for survival, and she was making her way. But Philip had shown her a life she had never experienced. A life with sailboats, fine dining and cashmere clothes.

Scanning the room, Jemma searched for Philip. Well-dressed women stood around the large room clinging to the arms of equally polished men. The ladies wore designer dresses meant to look casual and unpretentious, but the labels could have been on the outside. These women weren't fooling anyone.

Jemma glanced down at her plain print sheath adorned with a gold-plated necklace and button earrings. On her wrist hung a thin gold bracelet that she wore with pride. She eyed the lush, expensive jewelry weighting the necks and fingers of the other guests, and understood Philip's discomfort with her. How could he ever have Jemma on his arm?

She stiffened as feelings of inadequacy overwhelmed her. Stunned, Jemma spotted Philip with an attractive woman gripping his sleeve. The woman smiled into his face with a possessiveness that knifed Jemma's heart.

Just as she'd seen him do downstairs, Philip ambled among his guests, the perfect host. Occasionally, he paused to introduce the woman at this side. The couples shook her hand, gazing at her with admiration. After a polite moment, she and Philip moved on again, while Jemma's ache grew deeper.

Jemma turned away. Instead of feeling sorry for herself, she should rejoice for Philip. He'd been alone a long time. Companionship and love were God's gifts. Philip, who was so filled with compassion and thoughtfulness, deserved good things.

Planting a smile on her face, Jemma bandaged her

wound with determination. She'd prayed for guidance. She had to accept that this was God's will.
Other couples arrived, and Jemma directed them to
the hors d'oeuvres table before sinking back into her
thoughts.

Had she misread Philip? She'd assumed he didn't
have a special woman in his life. Any woman, for
that matter. When she really thought about it, she'd
misjudged his faith, too. He'd shown her and Claire
every gift of the spirit, every loving kindness. Maybe
Philip didn't attend church every week, but he knew
what God expected and he acted on it. Better than
she ever had.

"Would you like to mingle?" Ian said, stepping
to her side. "You look like you could use a break."

"I'm fine. Thanks." Jemma tried to send him a
sincere smile.

"At least get a plate of hors d'oeuvres. The crab
is wonderful."

She saw no sense in arguing. How could she explain?

With a forced thank-you, she headed across the
room to the large table spread with delicacies. Cav-
iar, fruit and cheese, finger foods of every description. Though the assortment looked tempting, her ap-
petite was fading as quickly as her hope.

Jemma forced herself to lift a crystal plate and
move along studying the array. Knowing she would
look foolish holding an empty dish, she speared a

piece of crab and a slab of melon—then froze when a familiar hand touched her arm.

"You look beautiful."

She lifted her eyes to Philip's longing gaze. "You're blind. Look at all the elegance." She motioned to the nearby crowd and noticed the woman who'd been on his arm now standing with a man and woman.

"Blind? Maybe I am." His expression was undefinable.

Flustered by his look, Jemma turned back to the table and lifted a strawberry onto her plate.

"Did you try the clam dip?"

His mundane question threw her off-kilter, and she eyed the table, expecting him to point it out. "No. Where is it?"

Instead, from his plate he lifted a cracker covered with the mixture and held it to her mouth. With their eyes riveted, she inched open her lips and he slid the appetizer between her teeth. The mixture of herbs and seafood played on her palate and wakened her taste buds. She slid her tongue over her lips to capture the crumbs. Philip's eyes held hers, and her heart stood still.

Tonight she knew for certain. She loved him. Perhaps she should feel anger or jealousy, but what she felt was longing. Locked in his gaze, Jemma stood like a shackled prisoner, unable to move.

"I'm a fool," Philip whispered as he reached forward and slipped the plate from her hand. In slow

motion, he set both plates on a tray and took her arm.
She walked beside him, wrapped in the lilting music
of the small ensemble, and when they reached the
parquet floor of the great room, he slipped his arm
around her back and drew her to his chest.

They moved as one, swaying and sliding, turning
and twirling, breathless and spellbound. Gliding in
rhythm, they seemed bound by a gossamer thread of
providence. Despite all that had transpired, Jemma
felt at home in Philip's arms.

Philip closed his eyes, facing an inner truth. No
matter what he'd tried to do—no matter how much
he had tried to spare Jemma and himself from hurt,
he'd failed. He'd been a fool to ask another woman
to be his date for the evening.

Jemma's cotton dress shifted beneath his fingers,
and Philip lingered on the softness of the cloth, imagining the softer skin beneath. Drawn by longing, he'd
taken her in his arms, knowing he had no business
tempting himself or her.

He'd sensed that she cared for him. And the fear
of hurting her pierced his thoughts. That's perhaps
what he feared the most. Yet what had he done this
evening? Her face had said it all. He was a fool. He
should let her go. Let her live. Philip fought his own
emotions. A little hurt now would save her from a
deeper wound. He scanned the room over Jemma's
shoulder and caught Ian's eye.

With an understanding nod, Ian moved across the
floor and tapped Philip's shoulder. "Do you mind?"

''No, not at all,'' he said, fabricating his response and his gracious smile.

Jemma's expression knifed his heart. He'd insulted her by giving her away so easily. More thoughtlessness.

Philip's hands trembled as he shoved them in his pockets and hurried across the room to the French doors that opened to the balcony. His date wouldn't miss him. He stepped through the opening, dragging air into his burning lungs.

When he looked up, he realized he wasn't alone. A few couples were bracing their backs against the wall or leaning against the balustrade. In the dim light, he eyed his wristwatch and realized the time. They were waiting for the fireworks display from the waterfront grandstands—a magnificent sight from his apartment.

Remembering his etiquette, he stepped back through the door and invited the others to join him outside. His guests followed his lead and drifted onto the terrace or stopped in the doorway. Philip waited as his date headed toward him, then he guided her to the railing with a vague excuse for his absence.

Unable to concentrate, Philip gripped the balustrade until Ian's voice sounded behind him. He glanced over his shoulder and saw Jemma, buried in the crowd, too short to view the display. Philip shifted sideways to make room, and Ian encouraged Jemma forward. Her perfume rose on the air and wrapped around Philip's heart.

Silent, she stood with her hands clasped to the handrail until the first colorful shower lit the sky. She gasped, and he saw her face light as brilliantly as the heavens.

One after another, the colors burst into the darkness, spiraling hissing tendrils and dazzling strands blossoming into shapes like red and orange chrysanthemums. Sprays of gold dust sprinkled from the sky.

Philip's guests fluttered with pleasure, and his date captured his arm, murmuring her delight. But Philip's hearing and sight were mesmerized by the petite woman in front of him.

With a quick apology, Philip edged away from his date and left the balcony. Inside the room, away from his guests and alone with his thoughts, he knew he needed to make a prayerful decision. Either stay away from Jemma or admit he loved her. He'd never known such deep longing as that which lured him to her side. Yet, a soft unwanted voice urged him to resist her charm...for her sake.

Jemma tucked her notes inside her case and leaned back in Ian's luxury car. They'd been involved in Philip's research for nearly two weeks. How many more resorts would they visit? How many brochures and pamphlets would they scour for tidbits of information? But she had one more idea of her own.

Turning to share her thought with Ian, she stopped herself. No, not Ian. She wanted to talk it over with Philip. He'd avoided her since the fireworks—since even before then. For a while the situation had roused her jealousy. She'd thought negative things, but then, she'd thought again. Even though he'd been with another woman, Jemma believed in her heart that he'd wished he were with her.

Each day her mind drifted back to the music and to Philip's arms around her, his gentle touch against her back, the shiver of yearning in his eyes. He was fighting his feelings. She sensed it. Was it her lack of education and money? Whatever it was, his absence pressed against her mind and dampened her spirit. She could handle it no longer.

"Let's stop for a drink and toss around some ideas," Ian suggested.

Jemma grasped for an excuse—even a lame one. "It's been a long day. Aren't you tired?"

"Not really. Are you? Coffee will give you a little oomph." He flashed her a friendly smile. "Work and no play isn't good. And you work too hard...for what?"

"The same reason as you, Ian," she said, wanting to shift the focus of the conversation. "You should be out enjoying yourself instead of working so many hours."

He chuckled. "I am trying to enjoy myself...if you'd let me."

Surprised at his bluntness, she looked at him and noticed a flush of discomfort. Her guilt got the better of her. "Sure, that would be nice. I'd like some coffee."

He pushed up his glasses and gave her a grateful smile.

Jemma had seen it coming—Philip pushing her and Ian together, concocting team projects like this. Did he actually believe that he could dupe her into falling in love with his assistant? If so, Philip Somerville had another think coming.

She was positive Ian had no idea what Philip had contrived. Though he was a good-looking man, Ian seemed somewhat of a loner. Not a recluse, but a man on the fringe of things. A thinker. A planner. Reading a book or browsing the Internet seemed more Ian's style.

Jemma had watched him in action these past weeks. He hovered in the background, keeping a low profile. When they'd visited the other resorts, she'd been the one to step forward to interview the desk managers and rooms supervisors. Ian took notes and remained the quiet spectator.

Now she feared Ian had deluded himself into thinking she might be interested in him—or that he was interested in her. Poor Ian didn't know his own mind.

A despicable idea drifted into her mind. A shameful plan that might teach Philip a lesson. She wondered what God would think of her now? Since Philip had manipulated this pitiful attempt at a romance between her and Ian, what would he do if he thought his plan had been successful?

Jemma was desperate, but she needed to think. Misleading Ian wasn't what she wanted to do, but maybe…just maybe she could find a way to force Philip to realize how much she meant to him.

Chapter Nine

Mottled August sunlight flashed through the window as Ian drove along the tree-lined highway. On the outskirts of Spring Lake, Ian pulled into a restaurant parking lot. Exiting, he came around to open Jemma's door. She followed him inside, dragging along her notes since he'd suggested they talk.

The menu listed the typical small-diner fare, but the desserts caught her fancy. One day she'd find herself too big for her sheath dresses and then she'd be in trouble, but until then, Jemma loved a good piece of cream pie.

"Coconut cream," she said to the waitress, and Ian ordered chocolate cake. The woman returned in a moment with two steaming coffees.

They sipped their drinks and chatted until the desserts appeared, then concentrated on eating.

Finally Jemma pushed away her empty plate and

pulled out her notes. "Do you want to go over this now?"

Ian looked surprised and fingered the edge of his eyeglass frames before answering. "I forgot my notes, but go ahead. What are you thinking?"

She rattled off her likes and dislikes. Eventually, they both agreed that nothing had crossed their paths but twists on what they'd already implemented.

"I'm not sure what Philip is looking for," Ian admitted. "The only thing he told me was that the resort has to keep growing."

"Why?"

His head jerked upward. "I don't know."

"I think the business is good. More clientele than we can handle most of the time," Jemma said. "You'd think Philip would want to enjoy a quiet winter. He could rev up for the busy summer."

"You'd think," Ian agreed.

"Does Philip travel?"

"Sails once in a while."

"That's not traveling," she said. "I meant to Europe or somewhere exotic."

Ian shook his head. "Philip sticks close to home."

"He should take a cruise to an exotic island. Run along a quiet stretch of sand, drink in the sun, get a tan." Her heart skipped as she envisioned Philip lolling on the beach beneath a stand of palm trees. She pictured herself cradled in a net hammock, swaying in a tropical breeze.

"A cruise would be nice," Ian said.

His comment jerked her from the enchanting fantasy, and he gave her a puzzled look.

Embarrassed at being so distracted, she apologized. "I was daydreaming."

"I figured," he said.

"Has Philip dated much?" The words were out before she could stop herself. She peered at Ian's knowing face. She was being too obvious.

"You mean, since Susan died?"

"Naturally," Jemma said, then immediately felt sorry for her brusque tone. "I doubt that he dated before that."

"Right." He sent her a foolish grin. "Not...until the last party. He was devoted to...well, he was always at the resort."

Ian's words sent a ripple of concern through Jemma. What had caused Philip to ask a woman to the party? Had Jemma sent him a message that she was chasing him? Was the woman his self-defense? She hoped that wasn't it.

She realized Philip was tied to the resort. He'd told her himself that he was married to his work. But Jemma didn't think he was anymore. His work ethic had become a habit, and she didn't believe that he loved it as he once had.

Jemma sensed a hunger in Philip, an emptiness that she wasn't sure he understood—but she saw it. He wanted more from life. And Jemma wanted to be the one to give it to him.

* * *

Philip looked toward the doorway. Where was Jemma? She was always on time. He turned back to Ian. "So how are things going with you and Jemma?"

Ian shifted in his chair, then pulled off his glasses and rubbed the bridge of his nose. "Okay, I suppose. We're not learning much that we didn't already know."

"Really?" Philip said, realizing his question had missed the mark. He rose and came around the desk, deciding to get to the point. "How have you two gotten along?"

Ian jammed on his glasses, his answer slow in coming. "Okay. Although, she spends the whole time talking about—"

"Can I come in?"

Both sets of eyes turned to the doorway. Jemma stood in the threshold, one hand holding her notes and the other clasped around the doorknob.

"Sure. We've been waiting for you." Philip gestured to the empty spot as he walked behind his desk. "Have a seat."

Jemma gave Ian a warm smile and eased into the chair.

Philip watched as she smoothed her skirt, adjusted the hem and crossed her slender legs.

"Well, now," he said, guilt rising up his neck as if he were a voyeur. "I suppose we can begin." He dropped into his chair.

Ian flipped through his notes, appearing to avoid

direct eye contact. Finally, he settled on a page and looked up. "Oh, are you waiting for me?"

"Either one of you," Philip said, feeling like a reveler who'd arrived too late for the parade. Since Jemma had entered the room, Philip had felt a strange uneasiness, and wondered why.

Ian didn't responded, so Philip turned to Jemma. "What did you think? Anything unique we might want to consider?"

"Not really. Ian and I've spent a lot of time together—" she sent Ian a sweet smile "—and both of us agree that Bay Breeze is tops."

"Really?" Philip didn't like the smile; nor did he like the goofy expression Ian had on his face. "You both agree, then?"

Ian nodded. "Jemma said it all. We reviewed our notes the other night and—"

"The other night?" To Philip's dismay, he had verbalized his thoughts. "You mean here?"

Ian fidgeted. "No, well, uh, we were—"

"If you're asking where we talked," Jemma said, "I think *that* evening we ate at a little café on Spring Lake. Isn't that where we were, Ian?"

"Right," he said, fidgeting with his glasses frame.

"A café?"

"If you're concerned about overtime, Philip, it was after work," Jemma said.

Philip shot from his chair, cringing at his ridiculous jealousy. "No, no. I was only thinking...that

I've worked both of you far too hard on this project." The lie rolled off his tongue.

"No problem," Ian said, "it's been fun."

"Yes, but…we've done enough researching, I think. You both seem to agree that we—" Philip faltered, realizing he'd been pacing in front of his desk. Where was his mind? Instead of fretting, he should be pleased that they'd fallen so easily for his plan.

Jemma lowered her head, attempting to hide a grin. A scowl distorted Philip's good looks, and watching him pace like a distraught lawyer filled her with delight…along with a smidgeon of guilt. Still, he deserved every minute of it.

Ian had jumped into the conversation, piling on details without any knowledge of Jemma's strategy. She couldn't have rehearsed him better.

Philip clamped his hands behind his back, and Jemma noticed a tic in his clamped jaw. "I suppose we're finished…if you have nothing new to add."

"It was a waste of time, really," Jemma said.

Seeming on edge, Ian rose. "If that's it, I'll get back." He strode toward the door, then paused and focused on Jemma. "Are you coming?"

"You go ahead, Ian."

He hesitated a moment, then turned and left the office.

Jemma rose, feeling awkward and miserable. Her emotions, she was sure, had emblazoned themselves on her face. But when she gathered the courage to look at Philip, he didn't seem to have noticed her discomfort.

"I'm glad…I mean, it's nice that you and Ian are, uh, becoming such…good friends," Philip said, his hands jammed in his pants pockets. "You need to have fun, Jemma."

"I manage," she said, wanting to fall on her knees and confess her terrible lie.

"How's Claire?" He pulled his hands from his pockets and folded them in front of him.

"She seems fine. She mentioned calling you one of these days." Jemma prayed Claire wouldn't forget.

"I've meant to call her."

"Now that I'm in the flat, I don't see her that often myself. Last Sunday we went to church together."

"Church…that's a place I haven't been in a long time. I joined United a long time ago, but it's difficult to escape this place on Sunday mornings."

Jemma studied his face, wondering if it was only an excuse or if Philip really meant what he said. Lyle had so often handed people a line. He had sounded like a deacon, but Jemma had realized finally that Lyle didn't know the Lord at all. With Philip, time would tell, and in the meantime, she'd pray.

Tension seemed to slip away from Philip's shoulders, and he motioned for her to sit again. He moved to her side and sank into the chair Ian had occupied, resting his elbows on his knees and folding his hands again. "I'm sorry that I sent you and Ian out on a wild-goose chase. I suppose it was silly."

"It's not a problem. I enjoyed seeing some of the other resorts, and I meant what I said. Bay Breeze is tops. We have nice rooms, great views, a sandy beach, and so many other activities. You hardly need to worry about all the other amenities I suggested."

"It sounds nice to hear you say 'we.' You've added some interesting features, but I feel I'm wasting your time here."

She grinned. "Where else would I be? At Claire's boutique?"

"At Jemma's boutique." He reached over and cupped her hand in his. "That's what you deserve."

"You're not going to offer to buy me a boutique, are you?" She arched an eyebrow to make a point.

"No. I'm a slow learner, but I'm not stupid."

Jemma chuckled. "By the way, I do have another idea. One I thought of before the 'goose chases.'"

"You do? You amaze me."

His tender smile stirred Jemma's heart. Rather than letting her emotions get carried away, she forced herself to be lighthearted. "I bet you're happy that other guy left."

"Other guy?" He looked at her curiously.

"The person who had my job before me. Did you forget?"

He lowered his eyes, and something niggled. "Is something wrong?"

"No, nothing. What's your new idea?"

She laughed at the enthusiasm in his voice and hurried to tell him about her good-morning basket idea—but she didn't want his approval as her employer.

She wanted Philip...to have and to hold.

Philip pressed the telephone to his ear, filled with disappointment. "I'm sorry, Claire, I'm sure the concert will be nice, but I really can't join you."

"Oh," Claire said, her disappointment evident in her tone, "I'd hoped you could. I don't see much of you."

With her comment, she'd tugged on his guilt. "This time of year is terribly busy...and if you hadn't been under the weather, I would have seen you at my Fourth of July party."

"I know," Claire said, "but that was mainly business, anyway."

He chuckled, hearing how right she was. "Yes, good public relations, Claire. You know about that."

"Maybe you could come by next week for cake. It's Jemma's birthday."

Jemma's birthday. Philip absorbed the information.

"Like she put it last Sunday," Claire continued, "when I asked her why she was moping around. 'In two weeks, I'll be thirty-three going on thirteen.' She believes everyone thinks of her as a child."

Her sentence jabbed Philip's consciousness. Hadn't he let Jemma know that he'd been wrong?

Didn't she realize in his eyes she was a desirable woman? A woman too tempting for her own good...for *his* own good.

Philip's chest tightened. Only thirty-three. The difference in their ages struck him again. Seventeen years. An impossible time span. But knowing it was Jemma's birthday, he was led to do something. "What's the date?"

"Date?" Claire's puzzled voice met his ear.

"Her birthday? Shouldn't we do something special?"

"Oh, it's August tenth, This Friday." A pause filled the line, then Claire spoke. "I suppose I ought to do something more than cake."

"I said *us,* Claire. Have you ever been out on a boat? How about a day sailing?"

"Me? On a boat? I can't imagine it, Philip. I'd be seasick, I'm sure."

"Oh," he said, hoping his disappointment wasn't too obvious.

"But don't let me stop you. Why don't the two of you go alone. Jemma would love it."

The picture sent Philip's heart on a gallop. Alone with Jemma on the boat for the entire evening...he couldn't trust himself. Not anymore.

"Let me give it some thought, Claire. Maybe we could combine a sail with dinner later and you could join us."

"Now that sounds like something I could handle," she said.

After promising to call her back when he'd made arrangements, Philip hung up the telephone. His mind snapped with ideas and concerns. If he took Jemma out on the boat and arranged for someone to bring Claire to dinner, who could he trust? Who wouldn't make too much out of his relationship with Jemma?

There was only one possible person.

Concerned, Jemma stood outside Philip's office door. He'd sent for her, and now she wondered if he'd changed his mind since their last conversation. She hadn't implemented her newest idea yet; she was still waiting for the baskets. But once they were in, she'd have a basket outside every room in the morning filled with doughnuts or sweet rolls, the morning newspaper, and juice. No other resort treated their guests as well.

In the outer office, Philip's secretary waved her through. But at Philip's door, she tapped first and waited to be admitted. Around him, her confidence always seemed to fade.

When she heard Philip respond, she pushed open the door.

"Jemma," he said, rising.

He gestured toward a chair across from his desk. She crossed the oriental carpet and sat.

"How are the morning baskets going?" he asked, settling into his desk chair.

"I ordered them." She eyed him, wondering if he

would give her a warning before putting the ax to her latest idea. "I can't do anything until they're in."

"Right. It shouldn't be long, then." He settled into his desk chair and smiled at her. "Every time I look at those logo mugs, I'm amazed. I'm not sure why we didn't think of something like that earlier. And what's a resort without fresh flowers in every room?"

"The bouquets are lasting at least three days. That's what the florist guaranteed. I've asked the housekeepers to pluck out the dead blossoms and—"

"You've thought of everything." Philip rose and came around the desk toward her.

Nerves prickled on the back of her neck. Anxious, she followed him with her eyes.

He stopped in front of the desk. "Why do you look so nervous?"

"I'm, uh, well, I thought something must be wrong."

He stepped forward and knelt beside her. "You're such a worrier. Don't assume that life is always lemons."

Seeing his face fill with sadness, her stomach knotted. "It's been nice lately."

"Then, why worry?"

She didn't know why. Though he obviously wasn't planning to cancel her morning-basket idea, she was still in the dark. "I don't think you called me in to tell me you're amazed by the logo mugs."

Philip laughed and shook his head. "No. I wanted

to tell you that I've planned—I should say Claire and I have planned—something for your birthday.''

Her birthday? She was surprised and curious. ''But why?'' she asked, wondering what was so special about being thirty-three.

''Why?'' He gaped at her. ''Must we have a reason to celebrate your birthday?''

She should have said thank you. Mortified at her reaction, she shook her head. ''No, but my birthday's never been a special occasion.''

''Well, it is now.'' He moved forward and brushed her cheek with the back of his hand. ''You're not working Friday.''

''I'm not?''

He nodded. ''Claire has all the instructions. Just do what she says.''

''Is she included in the plans?''

''How could we celebrate without Claire?'' He sent her a playful smile.

His good humor made her feel more balanced. She grinned back. ''You're right. What's a party without one of Claire's wild getups?''

Chapter Ten

Philip couldn't erase the pleasure from his face. His silly grin had been there since he'd picked up Jemma at the apartment. Why hadn't he done this before? Why hadn't he allowed himself to enjoy the pleasurable emotions that fluttered like a summer butterfly in his chest? He knew, but today he didn't care.

Like a double agent, he'd coerced Claire to use Jemma's extra key and sneak over to her apartment to pack some of Jemma's belongings for the birthday surprise. When she'd given the bag to Philip, he'd loaded the sloop with that and everything he thought they would need.

Today Jemma's confused expression added to his amusement. Trying to force Claire to join them, Jemma had finally yielded to leave her behind—with the promise she would join them later.

For fear of rumors, Philip had sailed the boat to

the municipal pier. Ever since Jemma mentioned her co-worker's peculiar looks, Philip had been fearful. He would never worry about the staff's gossip for himself, but he wanted no one to hurt Jemma—or tell her the truth about her job at the resort—until he decided a way to do it gently.

That guilt niggled daily. Philip realized, after the fact, that he should have been honest with her and explained he'd created the job especially for her. He wanted only the best for Jemma. Since her ideas were new, so was the position. It made sense. Instead, he'd hidden the truth and one day, he feared, he would reap the consequences.

When he parked at the municipal marina, Jemma did a double take. "We're sailing?"

"Sure are."

"Then, I know why Claire didn't come along."

He grinned. "You guessed it. She mentioned she'd be seasick." He slid from the car.

"But why is the boat docked here?"

"No special reason," he said, covering the truth. To halt any more questions, he closed his door, rounded the car and helped her out.

As they headed toward the sloop, he rattled on about the history of the municipal peer—anything to keep her mind busy while he mentally planned the rest of the day.

He might have been more comfortable with Claire along, knowing that he would have to be on his best behavior. But he'd promised himself that with Claire or without, Philip Somerville would be a gentleman. Still, promises were sometimes broken, and since he'd thrown his caution out the window, his imagination had conjured up a thousand romantic scenarios.

Philip motored away from the marina and headed down the river. When he'd made headway toward the mouth of the lake, going into the wind, he put Jemma at the helm while he hauled up the mainsail.

He couldn't have chosen a more perfect day. The sun burned in a cloudless sky and a steady breeze sent them over the water at an easy clip. At the wheel again, Philip looked over his shoulder at the vanishing shoreline, now only a ribbon of color on the horizon.

Claire had done her job. She'd seen to it that Jemma dressed in shorts and sleeveless top, just right for the day. Wearing oversize sunglasses, Jemma had stretched out on the cushion, her legs and arms bared to the sun, her posture the epitome of relaxation.

"You look too comfortable," Philip said. "Want to come back here and give me a break?"

"Sorry, I can't. Today's my birthday." Her generous lips curved to a teasing smile.

She looked totally content, and Philip tucked the image into his memory, wanting to hold each warm and comforting moment close to his heart.

Blanketed in sunshine, he headed farther onto the lake, until the horizon was a sheet of blue in every direction. Occasionally, a small triangle of sail appeared for a moment, then sank into the distance.

Deciding it was time, Philip lowered the sail and dropped anchor, while Jemma questioned him like a police detective.

To keep her quiet, he gestured toward the companionway. "Go down and put on your swimsuit."

"My what?"

"You heard me," he said. "It's on the bunk. Claire took care of you."

Jemma narrowed her eyes, but kept quiet and vanished down the ladder.

Beneath his clothing, Philip had worn his bathing trunks. He slipped off his walking shorts and tossed them on the bench. Reaching beneath the seat, he pulled out the wooden ladder and hooked it over the rail.

Anxious for a swim, he pulled his knit shirt over his head and looked down at the dark hairs bristling across his chest, thankful that the hoarfrost glinted only on his head. He pictured Jemma's golden, untarnished tresses. Why did he torment himself?

Hearing Jemma's return, he pushed his negative thoughts aside and motioned her to the ladder. "You can swim, I hope."

She gave him a grin. "A little late to ask me now, don't you think?"

"I figured Claire would've warned me when I told her to pack your bathing suit." He allowed his gaze to drift over her shapely frame—flawless trim legs rising to a slender, supple body wrapped in an electric-blue bathing suit. Perfect and beautiful.

"You trusted Claire?" she asked, her voice playful. "This might be her way to get me out of her hair...permanently."

She stepped onto the ladder, pivoted to face the lake, and dove like a knife into the glinting blue water. Fascinated, a sigh escaped Philip's chest. Jemma was every man's dream.

When she bobbed to the surface, Philip climbed down and joined her in the chilly water.

Side by side, they swam and jackknifed below the surface, then rose again, playing like dolphins. Emerging from below, the sun warmed Philip's arms and his heart thumped with the exercise and exhilaration.

"Enough?" he asked, gripping the ladder.

Jemma gave an agreeing nod and swam toward him. He helped her up and waited until she reached the top, then followed. On deck, Philip reached beneath the bench and pulled out two large towels. He tossed one to Jemma and wrapped the other around his shoulders, then pulled up the ladder.

The breeze played against his damp suit, and a chill bristled down his back. "Cold?" Bathed in water and sunshine, she sparkled like the morning dew.

"No, it feels wonderful."

Philip held his breath. She looked wonderful.

Holding the towel in front of her, Jemma tossed forward her shoulder-length hair and wrapped it in the terry-cloth. "I hope you thought of food." She held her hand against her flat tummy. "I hear a rumble, and it's not thunder."

"I think of everything," he said, hoping she would never know the thoughts firing his emotions.

He darted to the safety of the cabin, cooling his wayward thoughts. In a moment, he carried up the picnic basket he'd brought along, and they sat together on the bench enjoying slices of roasted chicken, slabs of cheese, crusty rolls and a variety of fresh vegetables and fruit.

"You do think of everything," Jemma said, licking her fingers and sending him a coy smile.

Hiding his desire, he opened a bottle of chilled Chablis, pouring it into the stemmed glasses he'd thought to tuck inside the basket.

When he handed a glass to Jemma, she raised it. "A toast."

"To your birthday." He held his glass even with hers.

"To my birthday...and to us."

The *tink* of crystal shivered in the air and in Philip's heart. *To us.* Her words bounced through his mind like a tennis ball. If his own fears would only let it be.

Jemma lowered her eyes, hearing her toast. *To us.* How could she have been so blatant? Sometimes she felt like a pendulum out of control. Her emotions swung back and forth, heading in wavering directions.

All day, she'd watched Philip at the helm, noticing his sunny smile, his attentiveness—just as he had been at the beginning. He'd mentioned his age so often since they met. Fifty. Why couldn't he see himself as he was? A handsome, vigorous man with more life than many men of thirty-three. What did he fear?

What did *she* fear? Her mind drifted back to the church concert that she and Claire had attended. Philip had said he was too busy. She'd been more than disappointed—she'd been uncertain and concerned. He'd said he was a Christian, but she truly wondered.

But today—right now—she felt wonderful. She pushed her concerns aside, praying that God would take care of her fear and find a way to make things right.

Sipping the Chablis, Jemma eyed him. "Why aren't you drinking your wine?"

"Boats and alcohol don't mix," he said. "I just wanted a sip to toast your birthday."

She was touched by his honest answer and concern for safety. She leaned back, other questions whirring in her head, and pondered if she should take a chance.

"Philip, why aren't we like this all the time?" she asked finally. "Being with you feels so good and natural. I couldn't ask for a better day."

Motionless, he studied her. "Do you want to know the truth?"

Her heart lurched, but she nodded.

"I don't want to lead you on, Jemma. Getting close and comfortable implies making promises. I don't know if the signals are different now than when I was—"

"Stop. I don't want to hear your young-old lecture again. Too many things are more important, Philip. Age is so minor." To her it was, but maybe for once she didn't understand him. "Is it more than age, Philip?"

Seeing the look on his face made her wonder if she'd made a mistake by asking, but she didn't stop. "Tell me what's bothering you."

He sat for a moment as if transfixed, then raised his head. "It's complex. Maybe it's not age so much as the ability to focus on what's important. It's being a husband and father. I ruined one woman's life and I won't do it again."

Jemma swallowed the gasp that had lodged in her throat. "Ruined? How? What do you mean?" Her mind soared with questions, with fears—she wanted to hear what he had to say, yet feared what he might say.

"You know how much time I spend in the office. Sometimes I'm there from morning to night." He dropped his napkin onto his lap. "I love my work, but a woman needs more. Young women need children. Susan needed more than I could give her. Sometimes I wonder…if God took her because I was doing such a pitiful job."

Jemma's head spun and color faded to black-and-white flashes. She gripped the railing. "Philip, you can't mean that. Men get even...not God. Do you hear what you're saying?"

"I shouldn't have said that. I'm sorry. I believed that once. Not anymore." He lowered his head and stared across the water.

"I don't want to hear that again. How can you say you don't give enough of yourself? Look at what you've done for Claire. And me. You helped Claire find a new fulfilled life for herself. You gave me a job and found that apartment for me. You're celebrating my birthday. You've taught me about sailing and...and living."

She saw his jaw flex with tension. His eyes remained distant.

"Maybe you were a workaholic once," Jemma continued. "Maybe you should have been a better husband for Susan." She clutched his arm until he raised his eyes to hers. "But it doesn't mean you can't be good for someone else."

He didn't speak, and Jemma didn't know what she would want him to say if he did. She swallowed a sob that shuddered in her throat.

She let go of his arm and her hand dropped to her lap. "Philip, if it's only friendship you want, then let's be friends. I enjoy your company. You've been kind to Claire and wonderful to me. I treasure you as a friend."

He pulled his gaze from the water, and his penetrating eyes sought hers. "I cherish you, Jemma. More than you'll ever know." His palm slid across the bench and captured her hand.

"Then, we've agreed," she said. "We're friends. Dear friends."

"The dearest."

With her hand in his, electricity rose up her arm, and she stopped breathing for a moment. Whatever Philip wanted to call it, Jemma would agree. He said they were the dearest friends. She called it love.

The candlelight twinkled in Philip's eyes, and Jemma struggled to keep her gaze from his. She tried to focus on Ian and Claire. Her mother-in-law's excitement bounced over the table, her mouth going a knot a minute. Jemma grinned inwardly at her play on words.

When she'd walked into the restaurant, Claire had sparkled in a floral sequin jacket covering her hot-pink gown. She glowed like a neon sign and with as much pizzazz.

Jemma's outfit was much more subdued. She gazed down at her plain white dress, thankful that Claire had used some discretion while packing for her surprise.

Claire had sent along a floral scarf, assuming, Jemma suspected, that she would wear it around her neck. Instead, Jemma had tied it around her waist like a sash, adding color without being too flamboyant.

Looking at the jewelry Claire had tossed in, Jemma had selected the large hoop earrings and a circular broach with colored stones that complemented the scarf. Despite Claire's wild taste, Jemma had made everything work well.

From the moment Philip had set sail back for shore, Jemma's head had been spinning. A damper had fallen on their conversation. If she'd been confused before about her relationship with Philip, she was doubly perplexed now.

Her mind drifted back to the table conversation. Claire had occupied Philip with tales of the shop and ideas for expanding the merchandise. Though quiet most of the time, Ian added a comment now and then.

The meal had been delicious, and the lobster bib had saved her from disaster. As they talked—and Ian smiled—the waiter gathered their empty plates and took a coffee order.

"You've enjoyed your day?" Ian asked.

"Yes, wonderful," Jemma answered.

"How far did you sail?" He drew off his eyeglasses, rubbed his nose and slid them on again.

"I'm not sure where we were." She eyed Philip, who was engulfed in Claire's story. "Philip dropped anchor, and we swam for a while, then had a picnic before sailing back."

His eyes widened. "A picnic?"

"On board. Philip thought of everything. Chicken, fruit…and wine."

"Hmm. Sounds very romantic."

It had been, until their conversation. But she chose not to respond. Let Ian figure it out himself.

"Would you like to dance?" Without waiting for her answer, he rose and extended his hand.

Jemma stared at it, realizing she could hardly refuse, but she didn't want to dance with Ian. She sent a helpless look to Philip, but Claire had his total attention.

With no other excuse, Jemma rose and allowed Ian to escort her to the dance floor and guide her into the rhythm of the ballad. He was shorter than Philip, but much taller than she. To answer his probing questions, she had to tilt her head to look into his face. Ian seemed a man for details. He delved into everything, and Jemma found herself providing information she would have preferred to keep to herself.

When the music stopped, Ian led her back to the table, apparently satisfied with the information he'd gleaned.

The coffee had arrived, and when she sat and lifted her cup for a sip, waiters appeared from every direction with a rousing chorus of "Happy Birthday" and a cake with lighted candles.

Uncomfortable with the attention, Jemma covered her burning cheeks and, eager to get rid of the crowd, blew out her candles and volunteered to cut the cake. When the waiters had left, she looked from Philip to Claire, wondering which one had arranged for her embarrassment. "Which one of you—"

"It was Claire's idea," Philip said with a twinkle

in his eyes, "but if she hadn't thought of it, I'm afraid I might have."

Giving a wry grin, Jemma slid the cake plate and knife toward Claire. "You started it, you finish it. Cut the cake."

During the quiet that accompanied Claire's concentration on the task, music drifted from the bandstand, and Jemma held her breath hoping that Ian wouldn't ask her to dance again. If he did, she'd tell him she didn't want to drink cold coffee.

"Philip, it's your turn," Claire said, using the knife as a pointer. "Dance with the birthday girl."

"Would you?" he asked, rising from his chair.

Cold coffee or not, Jemma didn't care. She stood and accepted his hand, and he walked her to the floor.

Always handsome, Philip was breathtaking tonight in his dark pinstriped suit. He drew her into his arms, and this time she allowed her body to meld with his, so close she could imagine the beating of his heart. He smelled of citrus and spice, and the aroma lured her into her old fantasy of a Caribbean grove of lemon and nutmeg trees. She closed her eyes, swaying like the island palms on a breezy afternoon, sun-warmed and unburdened.

Philip nestled her closer, his cheek against her hair, his hand caressing her back. Heat smoldered, then burst inside her chest and radiated through her limbs. She longed to raise on tiptoes and kiss his tempting mouth, to run her hand along his jaw and feel the growing stubble of his whiskers.

The music faded.

Philip slowed to a stop. Yet his arms kept her close, and Jemma feared he could feel the pulse of her blood racing through her veins. She tilted her head upward. His eyes glowed, and the dim light touched the silver in his hair.

"Thank you," he whispered.

I love you, her heart murmured in return, but her voice only whispered, "You're welcome."

Seventeen years meant nothing. Her heart thundered with conviction.

As if in slow motion, Philip guided her back to the table. Jemma nibbled on cake and sipped luke-warm coffee, her taste buds haunted by citrus trees and nutmeg.

When the bill was paid, they wandered back to Ian's luxury car. Though Philip insisted she slide into the front seat while he joined Claire in the back, Jemma didn't care. He was in her heart, no matter where she sat.

No one spoke until Ian stopped the car back at the marina.

Philip opened the door and spoke to her over the seat. "You can wait here while I get your things."

Jemma wasn't ready to say good-night. Her emotions cried for the night to go on forever. She flung open her door. "No, I'll go. I have things scattered all over." She gave a hurried look toward Ian. "Wait a minute. I'll be right back."

She darted through the parking lot with Philip behind her, her high-heeled sandals smacking the boards of the pier.

"What's the hurry?" Philip asked, grasping her arm.

She ignored him, afraid to look in his eyes, wanting to throw herself into his arms like a fool.

"Slow down before you get one of your heels caught between the planks. You'll be flat on your face."

She slowed.

Tenderly, Philip took her arm. When Ian's car had vanished from their sight, Philip slid his hand through hers, weaving their fingers together.

Her knees weakened as longing twined through her. She loved him.

Reaching the boat, Philip released her hand and took her elbow. "Careful in those shoes."

She stepped into the sailboat, slipped off her shoes and scurried down the steps into the cabin, hearing Philip behind her.

A hanging bag lay open on the bunk, and she opened the pockets and dropped her shorts and top inside, then went to the head for her wet bathing suit. Tugging it from the hook, she swung around—into Philip's arms.

The bathing suit dropped to the floor.

Music of the night filled her head. Swept with emotion, Jemma reached on tiptoe, wrapping her arms around Philip's strong neck, her mouth capturing his. Tenderly at first, he embraced her. Then his breath became gasps, and she felt him tremble.

Philip eased back, his lips moist and eager, and his eyes searched her face. He lowered his lips again, embracing her fully, lifting her. Mouth to mouth, yearning, joy beat through their veins.

He clung to her, and she to him—like swimmers drowning. Then, he eased her to the floor, and when she opened her eyes, his gaze looked misty and sad. "This isn't right, Jemma."

"What?" The word flew from her mouth. "This is beautiful, Philip. The day, the evening, and this."

"Beautiful, but…"

His reaction struck her like a slap. Why was it wrong? She'd already told him how she felt. Age meant nothing. She didn't understand. Humiliated, she backed away, grasped the bag and pushed past him toward the steps.

"Jemma, please, wait."

Maneuvering the bag through the narrow hatch, she bounded to the deck and onto the dock.

"Thank you for everything," she called over her shoulder.

"Jemma, please…"

Philip's voice faded with distance as her bare feet pounded against the pier.

She'd left her shoes—and her heart—behind.

Chapter Eleven

Philip watched her go, not knowing what to do to stop her. God knew he loved her, but he couldn't let go of his fear. How could he tell her he didn't want people to scorn her because of his age.

Cradle robber. He'd heard other men called that. Men who squired younger women. Married younger women. Jemma said seventeen years was nothing, but she was wrong. And he'd been a poor husband at thirty-three. Why would he be a better husband now?

Jemma needed a man with a future, and he'd told her so long ago that he was a man with an empty past. His life was in a horrible rut. Even before Susan died, he'd been there. One foot in the rut and the other on that banana peel?

He paused, his thoughts riddled with converging ideas. Could that banana peel be Jemma? Whenever

she was near—even the thought sent longing cours-
ing through him—he felt himself slipping. Out of
control. Or was it only his heart?

Tonight when he'd watched her dancing with Ian,
envy had torn through him. All day he'd been filled
with longing. He'd avoided being too close to her,
but Claire's suggestion that they dance left him little
choice. How could he not dance with Jemma on her
birthday? But once she was in his arms, he'd lost his
grip—lost his senses. He'd felt himself slipping, sliding, falling…in love.

He'd fought it too long. Why should he care what
others thought? If God had led him to Jemma, who
was he to oppose the Lord's will. Tonight he'd allowed himself to face the truth. He'd fallen in love.
And as much as he wished it didn't, it felt wonderful.

For three days Jemma dodged around corners at
the resort and at home, avoided answering her telephone, fearful of seeing or talking with Philip. What
would she do? He'd confused her beyond any hope
of understanding. His kiss had been as rapturous as
her own. Yet he had apologized. He'd said it was
wrong. Why?

She'd been a widow for two years. He'd been a
widower much longer. What would make a kiss
wrong for two consenting adults? Or had she been
the only one willing?

Reliving the moment, she remembered her arms
around his neck, her lips moving against his. She'd

been the first to embrace him, but he hadn't backed away. Instead, he'd swept her off the floor in his powerful arms. He'd felt what she had—she was sure of it. What would make that wrong?

In the back of her mind, she remembered something Philip had said that troubled her. What was it? She delved into the corners of her memory. *My Lady.* That was it.

A shiver had run down her back when he'd looked into her eyes and said that he figured after his wife's death the sailboat would be the only other ''she'' in his life. He'd even laughed at her. Was he that determined to remain alone? She didn't understand.

Jemma longed to talk with Claire, but she couldn't. Claire would get too involved, and she knew Jemma too well. When Jemma had returned to the car that night, Claire had seen her face and later wanted to know what was wrong. She'd pried for the past two days, but Jemma was determined to keep her feelings private. She wanted answers, but she needed time to struggle with the situation. Time to be alone.

Jemma stepped back from the polished table and scrutinized the flowers she'd placed in the pastel vase. She shifted a stem of daisies and eyed the mixed bouquet again, admiring how fresh and perky they looked. So full of life.

When she was with Philip, she felt like fresh flowers. New and promising. But today, she was as wilted as the dying blossoms she'd tossed into her trash bag. Cheerless.

A blast of air escaped her lungs. Today she had dragged herself through the guest rooms, time dragging along with her. She glanced at her wristwatch. "On to the next." Her voice sounded strange in the empty room. She grabbed the cart handle and swung toward the door. She came to an abrupt stop. "Philip."

"I found you," he said, standing at the threshold. He pushed the door closed behind him and headed toward her, his steps muffled by the carpet.

"What's wrong?"

"I'm wrong," he said. "I came to apologize."

"It's not necessary."

He caught her hand. "I didn't mean to upset you, Jemma. You're the dearest friend I have...and I don't want to lose you. I need to explain."

"You owe me nothing. I made a mistake." She tried to look into his eyes, but her focus remained on the floor.

He slipped his finger beneath her chin and lifted her face to his. "I made the mistake, not you."

She shook her head, unable to make sense out of what he was saying. "I don't understand."

"Let's be friends, Jemma."

Friends. Was that it? Philip truly thought of her as a friend. *Dear friends.* Nothing more? He could say it all he wanted; she didn't believe it. But even if he never realized how he felt, she'd never beg him to love her.

Philip glanced over his shoulder toward the door.

"We can't talk here," he said, swinging back to face her. "I'll pick you up tonight so we can sort things out. What do you say?"

As far as Jemma was concerned, they could sort things out until kingdom come and he'd still make no sense. What was wrong with loving, when your heart told you it was right?

"What do you say?" he repeated.

"I have plans tonight, Philip." She'd told him a barefaced lie. She glanced at her wristwatch. "Look. Time's fleeting. These flowers will be dead if you don't let me get them into vases."

"So be it. They'll die. You're more important."

His comment shocked and pleased her.

He captured her arm and pulled her close. "Forget your plans, please. Just say yes."

She looked in his desperate eyes and her heart ached. "All right."

He brushed her cheek with his fingers. "Thank you, Jemma." He took a step backward. "I'll pick you up around seven."

Before she could respond, he'd vanished through the doorway.

Philip bristled with determination. He refused to let things get out of hand tonight. Being in a restaurant would hopefully temper Jemma's irritation, and he could speak from his heart.

When he picked her up she seemed tense, but by the time they'd pulled into Bil-Mar's parking lot, she'd begun to relax. Inside, the hostess seated them on the open porch overlooking the lake.

"This is lovely," Jemma said, looking toward the diamond-studded ripples. "Must have cost you to get this table."

He grinned. "I told them that it was for you. I had no problem."

A soft flush highlighted her cheeks, and his spirit sparkled like the sun-speckled water.

The waiter arrived and took their order. They talked about many things, but nothing of importance. When the excellent meal had ended and coffee had been poured, Philip took Jemma's hand.

"Ready to talk?"

"Sure."

Her voice sounded tentative, and she lowered her eyes. With her free hand, she fiddled with her water glass, leaving damp rings on the tablecloth as she turned it. When she looked up, he saw concern in her eyes.

Philip shifted the tumbler aside and clasped both of her hands in his. "I know I upset you the other night when I said that our kiss was wrong."

She nodded.

"You asked why it was wrong. How could a kiss...so wonderful...be wrong?"

Her jaw tensed as she listened.

"The kiss wasn't wrong, but...I felt that I was wrong...for you."

"You're wrong for me?" Her face became distorted. "What are you telling me?"

From the look on her face, the conversation wasn't going as he wanted, but it was too late to turn back. "I'm not the best man for you, Jemma."

"You're telling me what's good for me?" Her back straightened as rigid as a post.

He squeezed her hands. "I know what you've said about age. But...we're talking about seventeen years. You're a young woman. When you're fifty, I'll be sixty-seven. Can't you understand that? I want you to have a wonderful life with a younger man—" he began to panic "—who'll give you children and won't die before they're out of high school."

She pulled her hands from his grasp and pressed them against the linen cloth. Clasping the table edge, Jemma lifted herself upward and jutted her face closer to his. "It's what *I* want, Philip, not what you want. Don't you understand?" Looking defeated, she sank back into the seat. "You can't decide my life for me."

Had he done it again—tried to force his ideas on her? He closed his eyes, hoping to calm his throbbing heart.

"Besides, I think you have that wrong. Are you talking about love and marriage?" she asked.

His eyelids snapped open, but she continued before he could find a response.

"I didn't ask you to love me...or marry me. A kiss is only a kiss."

"It was more than that to me," Philip murmured.

Jemma shook her head. "It's not a life commitment."

Her comment shocked him, and he scrambled to express his feelings. "But maybe it should be."

She leaned forward, her eyes narrowed. "Under whose rules?"

Philip opened his mouth, then closed it, wondering if again he was pushing his dogma on her. Like his father and Andrew, a fight to the finish. The comparison shot through him. But this was very different. Didn't Jemma hold the same beliefs that he did?

"You see. You have no answer. It's only how you see it."

A response tumbled from his mouth. "My rules...and God's."

"What do you mean?"

"I don't think God wants people to play with emotions. It's temptation."

"My kiss? Temptation? I'm luring you to sin?"

Her whisper hissed across the table, and he had no idea what to do or what to say. "I'm not accusing you. I'm blaming myself. I'm not perfect."

"You've made too much out of it, Philip."

"What do you mean?"

"The kiss was a thank-you...for your friendship and kindness. For my birthday surprise. Nothing more."

"Nothing more?" He remembered every detail, the sensations he'd felt, the look in her eyes. He fell back against the chair and peered at her. "No, Jemma, you're avoiding the truth."

Jemma looked at his face, the hurt in his eyes. She had not been honest—just as he'd said. Her argument was dashed to the ground. "Yes, I'm avoiding the truth." Her heart fluttered at her admission, but she felt calmer telling the truth.

The tension drained from his face and his mouth curved to a hesitant grin. "You're not saying that to make me happy, are you?"

She grinned and felt her spirit rise for the first time since they'd begun the conversation. His words from the past filled her mind. "You don't need me to make you happy. I'm sure happiness finds you."

His amused chuckle filled the air. "I deserved that," he said. He leaned forward and lowered his voice. "Let's get out of here."

She agreed. What they had to talk about needed to be finished in a different atmosphere.

Philip flagged the waiter and settled the bill, then rose and held her chair. She stood and followed him through the restaurant and back outside into the evening breeze.

"Come with me," he said, taking her hand as they passed through the parking lot and guiding her to the beach.

Sand filled her shoes and Jemma slipped them off, dropping them near the grass. In stockinged feet, she ran toward the water, letting the waves roll over her toes and drag the shifting earth back into the lake.

Philip caught her hand and drew her to his side. His eyes sparkled in the dusky light, and she longed to kiss him as she had done the night on the boat. He broke the mood by sliding his arm around her shoulder and moving along the shoreline.

With slow steps, they walked in silence along the sand, ignoring the water that spattered his pant legs and the hem of her dress.

When they'd wandered beyond the view of the restaurant porch, he stopped and faced her.

Jemma waited, her heart skipping like that of a child at recess. But she didn't move. Didn't give an inch.

His face filled with emotion—hunger, desire, pain, grief. A mixture Jemma didn't understand. His eyes captured hers while he slid his hand up her shoulder, along her jaw to her cheek. His fingers caressed her skin, then tilted her chin upward, and she watched his lips part as he eased his mouth onto hers.

She held her breath, enjoying the gentle touch, the eagerness of his mouth, his rapid breathing that filled her ears, louder than the rolling waves.

She caught her own breath as he pressed her against his trembling chest, exploring her back and arms with gentle caresses.

With a moan, Jemma yielded to his kiss, tossing her concerns aside and allowing her spirit to soar into the night sky.

When his shoulders relaxed and he drew away with tiny kisses to each lip, she opened her eyes. His smile weakened her knees, and she clung to him for support.

"This is right, Jemma. For all my fears and concerns, this must be right."

His last words melted to a sigh, and he kissed her and sent her heavenward again, her feet washed by the waves, her heart bathed in love, and her mind flooded with hope.

Philip stood outside the door, watching Jemma fill the new morning baskets. She lifted a checked gingham napkin and tucked it inside, slid in today's newspaper, two empty juice bottles, then stopped.

He grinned when she pulled everything out and started again. She was practicing, he knew, for the baskets' debut, and he was touched by her serious approach to the task.

Having made his decision after days of mental strain, Philip decided to test the waters of gossip. Always in the past, he'd avoided contact with Jemma at the resort, other than in the safety of his office. Only once, a few days ago in desperation, had he approached her as she worked.

But the time had come. He'd protected her long enough from rumors and disdainful looks. Since admitting to her and to himself how he felt, he had to be open—candid with the resort staff.

His explanation bothered him, and he wondered if he had been protecting more than Jemma. Had he feared the community's reaction to his December-

May romance? Was his pride and reputation holding him back from admitting how he felt?

The answer, in part, was yes. But now, he didn't care what anyone said. God was on his side, and if Jemma loved him, he wanted nothing more than to spend his life with her.

He touched the doorknob, and Jemma's eyes shifted toward the sound. When she saw him, a gentle flush rose up her neck, and he saw her look past him beyond his shoulder, afraid, he was sure, that someone would see him.

He pushed the door open wider and stepped inside. "Indecision or practicing?" He grinned at her expression.

"I want this to be perfect. I told Latrice and the foods manager that I'd train someone to handle this…so I have to know what I'm doing."

She draped the gingham over the basket edges again, tucked and poked the items, adding her imaginary sweet rolls, and topping the basket with two more colorful napkins. "There. What do you think?"

"It's almost as pretty as you are," he said, sliding his arm around her shoulder.

She pulled back and glanced toward the doorway. "Philip, please, someone will see you."

"Do I care?"

A puzzled look shot to her face. "I thought you did. Remember, discretion?"

"That was years ago," he said. Though their dinner at Bil-Mar's had been only four days earlier, it seemed he'd wanted to shout his feelings from the housetops forever.

She laughed and gave him a jab. "You have a warped sense of time."

He did. How long would it have taken for him to face his feelings and admit his personal fears? He loved this woman, and he'd yet to say the words aloud.

"I don't suppose you came in to watch me fill this basket, did you."

"No, I came by to invite you upstairs."

"Upstairs?" She tilted her head with a quizzical look. "Top floor?"

"Penthouse." He gave her a wink, and his pulse did a two-step.

"Now?"

"Tonight."

"Tonight?"

"Having problems with your hearing?"

"No, but...you mean in front of others. Should I stand at your private elevator? Or do you want me to take the emergency stairs?"

He laughed at her caution; she was nearly as bad as him. "I want you to wear a sign."

Her face brightened and his spirit soared. He backed away, his hand reaching for the doorknob. "I'll see you tonight."

She nodded.

"About seven?"

"Okay."

"And don't have dinner."

Chapter Twelve

Jemma felt shy standing in front of the bank of elevators. She could hardly believe that Philip had suggested she come up this evening. She'd only been in his apartment the night of the party. Never alone.

Nervous, she glanced over her shoulder, wondering if someone she knew might ask her what she was doing. What would she say? And how would they react?

The elevator chimed, and she entered, still not knowing the answers to her "what ifs." She pushed the top button. The door closed and the cage ascended, along with her jitters.

The door slid open and she stepped into Philip's foyer. Through the archway, she saw his reflection in the broad window. He turned at her footfall and came toward her. Her heels clicked on the marble flooring, and then she stepped into his open arms.

"Was it so bad?" he asked.

"No, just a little…weird." She tilted her head upward, and he pressed a quick kiss on the tip of her nose.

"Join me," he said, guiding her into the living room. "I poured some wine."

He led her to a large sofa and she sank into its deep cushions. Philip handed her a stemmed glass filled with a crystal-clear wine. She sipped and allowed the tang to lay on her tongue.

"Good?" Philip asked.

She nodded, though truly her judgment of wine was poor. Her past had offered little occasion for celebrating. The thought brought a question to mind. What special occasion were they toasting tonight?

Before she asked, a tantalizing aroma drifted into the room. She drew in the scent. "I smell something wonderful."

"Dinner," he said.

"It's here already?"

"Already?" He looked puzzled.

"From the kitchen. I assumed you have your meals sent up."

"You assume wrong, my dear. Tonight, I prepared this myself."

She fell against the sofa with a grin. "You?"

"I left my chef's cap in the kitchen." He rose and beckoned her. "You haven't seen my kitchen."

"I haven't," Jemma said, filled with curiosity. She had no idea if he was serious or teasing, but she followed, pattering behind him into a vast kitchen. Pure white cabinets, floor, walls, appliances.

"I'd never have the courage," she said, imagining the damage she could do to the pristine room.

"Soap and water works wonders," he said, grinning. "But you don't think I clean this place myself, do you?"

The luxury of having a housekeeper and a chef, she could only fantasize about. "What smells so delicious?"

"My specialty. Thick pork chops cooked in my own special sauce."

She laughed. "Your own special sauce! It sounds like a fast-food ad."

"Wait until you taste it."

He sent her back to the living room while he remained in the kitchen to finish the meal.

Jemma placed the goblet on a table and wandered through the open French doors. In the rosy glow of the setting sun, she saw the balcony for the first time unhampered by party-goers and darkness. She sat in a wrought-iron chair arranged beside a matching table, and looked out across the water. The view was beautiful—and so was the life, she imagined.

A few minutes later, Philip's call roused her from her chair and she headed back inside, following the enticing aroma to the dining room. In candlelight, she slivered tender pieces of pork and tasted his rice pilaf mingled with herbs. The meal was delicious—the company, exquisite.

"More Riesling?" he asked.

She nodded, and when he filled her glass, she asked the question that had occurred to her earlier. "What are we toasting? Anything special?"

His gentle smile warmed her more than the wine. "Very special." He lifted his glass.

"Give me a hint," she said, following his salute.

"To us."

The crystal tinkled at their touch.

Us. The sweet word fluttered through her chest. She recalled making that blatant toast on the boat, but this time the word wrapped around her heart. Still, she longed to know what he meant.

Jemma finished the scrumptious food quickly on her plate. She placed her knife and fork on the rim and folded her hands. "My compliments to the chef. This was exceptional."

"I'll give him your message, but we're not finished yet. Dessert and coffee will be served on the balcony."

Ignoring his protests, she carried the dishes into the kitchen, then he shooed her off while he finished. She wandered outside again, leaning on the railing and enjoying the August breeze. In moments, he came through the doorway.

"The coffee's on. I thought maybe you'd like to sit a while and watch the sunset."

"Yes, I would."

He slipped his arm around her waist and guided her to a cushioned bench.

Feeling more comfortable than she'd felt in years, Jemma nestled in the crook of Philip's arm and gazed at the glowing horizon as the fiery colors melted into the shimmering gold water. The brilliance couldn't hold a candle to the joy blazing in her heart.

Philip shifted, and she turned to him, sensing he wanted to talk.

"Could we go back in time and start again?"

"Back? How far?" She wondered what he was suggesting.

"Probably the first time I hesitated to do what my heart told me to do. That was about day two."

Heat warmed her cheeks, and she was pleased that the orange sky camouflaged her flush. "I can't bear to go that far back."

He couldn't bear to go back that far, either, but they had to. "How about the night on the boat?"

"What part of that night?"

He noticed her tender blush even in the glow of the setting sun. "The part where you kissed me."

"You mean you want me to—"

He nodded before she finished. She hesitated, shifting on the bench and sliding her hands along his arms, and his muscles tensed with anticipation. When she reached his neck, she lifted her hands and caressed his jaw, his cheek, and let her fingers play along his lips.

Longing rose in him at her touch. A flame kindled in his chest and spread to his limbs.

She tilted her full mouth toward his and slid her

hand to the back of his head, pulling him down to meet her lips.

In pure abandon, he surrendered. Jemma's stifled gasp melted to a moan, and Philip's hopes were answered. Her lips parted against his, the warmth radiating from her heart. He captured her against his chest, longing to make her his own.

Temptation. Like a neon sign, the word lit in his head and he warned his eager heart. He would do nothing to hurt her, nothing to destroy the purity of their love.

Jemma eased away, trembling and breathless, and for once he opened his heart and let out the words he'd hidden for so long.

"I love you, Jemma."

Surprise filled her face as she searched his eyes. "I love you, too," she said in a whisper. "I've never loved anyone as much."

His own thoughts echoed her words even as guilt and sorrow nipped at his conscience. He'd been unfair to Susan. He'd loved her, but not like this.

Jemma's expression told him she was sensing something wrong. "What is it?"

Weighing whether he was wise to tell her, he decided honesty was the beginning of a pure, untainted love. He'd messed up earlier with his evasiveness. Somewhere along the line, he needed to tell her the truth about her position at Bay Breeze. But not tonight. He wanted nothing to ruin this important moment.

"I was thinking about my relationship with Susan," he began. She listened as he poured out his heart, and he looked toward heaven, thanking God that Jemma seemed to understand.

When he had finished baring his soul, she kissed his cheek and then his lips. He turned her face toward him and kissed her moist eyes, his heart bursting with love.

"I was thinking as you talked," she said, "how we learn so much from experience. You're not alone, Philip. I made mistakes in my marriage—things I wish I could change. There are sorrows that I feel deep inside."

She slid into the crook of his arm and talked into the darkening sky.

"I don't know if things could have been different. Sometimes I think we tune out God and make our own decisions without his guidance. If I'd listened, I'm guessing the Lord would have told me marrying Lyle was a mistake."

He nodded thinking of his own experience, wondering if he, too, had tuned the Lord's voice from his mind and bungled along his own path.

"I don't know if Lyle was as miserable as I was. And you don't know about Susan. Maybe she accepted your marriage, like the vow 'for better or worse.' We never know which it will be, but we accept it. That's what I did."

Philip had done the same, but still felt he should have tried to make things better.

"'What ifs' aren't constructive," Jemma said.

His pulse surged at her comment, almost as if she'd heard his thought.

"What we need to hang on to is God's guidance. If you and I learned from our mistakes, we can be better marriage partners. We realized our mistakes, and we're repentant."

"And forgiven," he said, surprised that he'd spoken aloud.

"I think God's forgiveness is something you and I haven't accepted." She tilted her head and looked into his eyes.

"I think you're right."

"Does that mean we don't trust the Lord?"

Philip shook his head. "No, it's more like we feel unworthy."

"Yes, you're right."

Her soft laugh surprised him.

"How can we be unworthy," she asked, "when God created us and loves us? Even more than I love you…and you love me."

The concept was unbelievable. Philip rose, taking Jemma's hand and drawing her to his side. With his arm around her waist, he stepped toward the railing. "You're a true disciple, Jemma."

"Only inspired," she said.

He saw the love in her eyes and he knew they had so much more to talk about. He prayed they had a lifetime to do so.

* * *

Philip stood outside the Fellowship Church, surprised he'd agreed to attend. But he realized he was there for Jemma...and for himself.

Too much time had passed since he'd sat in the Lord's house and listened to God's Word. Philip believed, he prayed, he followed the commandments, but he didn't worship publicly. He'd tossed rationalizations around in his head often—time, inclination, lethargy.

When he did go to church, he would sit in the service and his mind would drift, planning the day's activities and solving his business problems. When the service was over, he felt no different than he had before he walked in—except maybe resentful for having wasted his time. Not resentful of God. God never wasted his time. God had provided him with gifts beyond his belief. But the *service* had wasted his time. He left feeling spiritless.

Attending this church today was important to Jemma, so it was important to Philip. And that's why he'd come with her despite his responsibility at the resort. Someone else would handle the crises.

"Come on," Jemma called, halfway up the stairs before he had stepped around the car.

Grinning at her eagerness, he helped Claire from the back seat, and she swept out, dressed in one of her colorful Indian print dresses.

"You're a vision, Claire," he said, taking her arm as they headed for Jemma.

"Seeing you here is a vision to me," she said with a soft chuckle.

Jemma waited at the door until Philip and Claire caught up with her. Her face glowed, and he wished he'd been more genuine with his faith sooner. Her questions about his belief had no doubt caused her concern. She deserved so much more.

As soon as Jemma opened the door, Philip heard the difference. Music from an organ and piano sailed to greet them with a spirited hymn. The vitality caught in his chest, and he looked around, amazed at the smiling faces that greeted them as they passed through the entrance to the worship area.

"Good morning," voices called, as he followed Jemma down the aisle to the front. Once they were seated, he peered through the morning program, reading lists of meetings and events, amazed at how active the congregation seemed.

The opening hymn brought him to his feet, and on all sides hands lifted in praise as voices rang through the sanctuary. When he was seated again, Bible verses were read, and the choir sang, filling his heart with unexpected comfort at their message.

Today he understood what it meant to praise. He heard it in their voices and saw it in their faces. Why hadn't he realized before that this is what he needed? He smiled, seeing how God works in mysterious ways, not only bringing Jemma into his life, but bringing Jemma's pure, simple wisdom into his heart.

When the preacher came forward for the sermon, Philip waited with curiosity. Would he drift off again to solve resort concerns…or think about the wonderful moments with Jemma in his arms? Even on a good day he had a difficult time keeping thoughts of Jemma from occupying him.

The pastor opened the Bible and looked at the congregation. "Listen to God's Word from the third chapter of Proverbs. 'Blessed is the man who finds wisdom, the man who gains understanding, for she is more profitable than silver and yields better returns than gold. She is more precious than rubies—nothing you desire can compare with her.'"

Gooseflesh rose on Philip's arms. *Wisdom.* He felt the soft flesh of Jemma's arm beside his, her eyes directed at the preacher. Jemma had become Philip's wisdom, telling him that age didn't matter, that the important thing in life was learning from experience to be a better Christian and a more loving mate.

She is more precious than rubies; nothing you desire can compare with her. His heartbeat quickened, and he slid his hand to hers, winding their fingers together as one. He needed to know this wasn't a dream—that it was real.

Philip felt her warmth against his hand, the blood pumping through her veins. She turned once and sent him a smile that anchored him to the truth. Young or old, God had meant for them to be together.

And what was seventeen years? A heartbeat in God's time. They would manage…more than manage. They would live and be a family. And if Jemma wanted children, then…he would be a good father. He imagined himself at fifty-five or fifty-six playing ball with a young son, combing a little girl's hair. The picture hung in his thoughts, alien but sublime. He sensed this was God's plan for him and prayed that Jemma was hearing the same message.

When the service ended, Philip knew he would come back to worship, and he understood why Jemma had brought him here—God's wisdom. Some people moved down the aisle, some exited the church, others came forward to pray.

He followed Jemma outside, feeling alive and spirit-filled. On the sidewalk, Jemma and Claire introduced him to friendly faces, people whose names he didn't remember and whose words he couldn't recall. All that clung to his thoughts was that God understood his fears and had spoken to him through the Word.

"What did you think?" Jemma asked when they reached the car.

"Very nice," he said. "I know why you wanted me to come. Thanks."

Jemma didn't ask him to explain, and although he sensed Claire's eagerness to grill him, she used good sense and remained quiet. When they pulled up at Claire's, he declined her invitation for coffee. He needed to get back to work, but more, he needed time to think. Time to find the perfect way to confess his dishonesty about Jemma's position, and tell her how much she'd changed his life.

Chapter Thirteen

Looking down the leaf-strewn path, Jemma ran ahead of Philip, her laughter sailing behind her. She couldn't wait to see the overlook that offered a view of the sand dunes and Lake Michigan.

Jemma's heart swelled as she breathed in the pungent September air. She'd never felt as carefree and as loved as she had during the past few weeks.

"Hurry," she called, glancing over her shoulder and motioning.

"Wait up," Philip said. "Give a guy a chance to breathe."

She dashed away again, her feet dancing through the colorful autumn leaves that covered the path and canopied the sky overhead. Red and gold shimmered with sunlight, contrasting with the spindly evergreens that clung with shallow roots to the sandy floor.

Philip stopped and spread out his arms. "Have mercy," he said, his laughter punctuated by gasps.

Jemma spun around and raced back, bounding into his embrace and wrapping her eager arms around his neck.

He kissed her nose and chin, then slid her to the ground. "You have to remember a reality, my lady—" along with the nickname he flashed her a sly smile "—seventeen years does have its drawbacks."

Jemma laughed and tucked her arm around his waist. Lately, he'd been a good sport about the age difference and she tried to be patient. He'd made a positive improvement.

Ahead, Jemma saw the trail open and she pulled away. "Sorry. I can't wait," she said, running backward for a moment before she spun around and darted ahead.

The sight was awesome. Rolling dunes stubbled with beach grass, silverweed and beach peas extended down to the bright blue water.

In seconds, Philip reached her side and leaned against the railing. "What do you think?"

"God's world. When you see raw nature, you wonder how people can question whether or not there's a God."

He nodded and slipped his arm around her shoulder. "And the scenery's almost as perfect and beautiful as you are."

She started to disagree or give him a playful poke,

but she stopped herself. Sweet words and tenderness were something new to her, something she needed to learn to welcome. She'd never had another man make her feel so cherished.

When she had taken in all she could of the quiet loveliness of the surroundings, she nudged Philip forward, anxious to see more of the park.

Arm in arm, they followed the path in silence. Only the snap of a twig, the rustle of leaves or a bird call pierced the hush of the woods.

"This is the best time of year to follow the trails, I think." She dipped down and gathered a handful of fallen leaves, holding them out in front of her. "When else can you find a full palette of color?"

He grinned, and she sensed he was about to tell her he saw it in her eyes or in her heart. Instead, he nestled her closer and remained silent.

She scattered the leaves along the path until he drew her to a stop.

"What is it?" she asked.

He tapped the side of his head with his index finger. "Forgetful. I've been meaning to ask you if you'd be my date for the Chamber of Commerce fall icebreaker."

She looked at his face, trying to read his expression. "Icebreaker? What's that?"

"It's just a get-together like an open house, to invite new businesses in the community to get involved with the Chamber of Commerce. It's casual. No big deal, really."

His unexpected invitation was a big deal to her. He'd never asked her to be his escort before, and her shoulders tensed.

He must have noticed because he lifted his hands and kneaded the muscles above her shoulder blades.

"You'd do me a favor," he said. "I'd like you to go with me."

She spun around and faced him. "Are you sure? You don't have to do this."

His eyes filled with tenderness. "I know I don't. I want to. It's time I introduced the world to the woman I love."

She drew in a shuddered breath, knowing how difficult this was for him. "I love you, but..." She searched his eyes for the truth. "Yes, I'd love to be your date."

He pulled her against his chest, then took her hand and they headed off again. After only a few yards, they reached the visitor center and stopped near the building.

"You've already been inside the center." Philip tucked his hands in his windbreaker. "What do you think? Ready to go?"

She looked overhead at the powder-blue sky. Never. Today was too glorious to sit in her flat or at Philip's. Nowhere had she seen such an abundance of autumn colors and glorious sunshine. "Must we?"

He chuckled. "No. What do you have in mind?"

His tone left a double-sided question. What did *he* have in mind? Grinning, Jemma tugged from her pocket a folded brochure that she'd found inside the center and scanned the map.

Philip studied the park layout over her shoulder. "Well, what do you wish?" he asked, whispering the *W* sounds against her neck.

Pressing her jaw to her shoulder to stop the tickle, she giggled, then spun around, her brochure flapping in the breeze. "Let's go to the picnic area and...do anything. Play catch?"

He shrugged and shook his head. "No ball." But in a flash, he gave her a thoughtful scowl and headed for the car. He lifted the trunk, reached inside, then turned toward her waving a Frisbee.

"Wonderful." She left the visitor center sidewalk and crossed the parking lot to his side.

"Someone left this at a Chamber of Commerce picnic a couple years ago. No one claimed ownership, so I tossed it in the trunk. Who'd know it would find a use?"

Playfully, she rolled her eyes. "God."

Philip knew she was right. He'd finally accepted that God was in charge. With Jemma's hand tucked in his, they continued down the path toward the picnic area. He found the walk faster along the asphalt road.

In a few minutes they arrived, and Philip peered beyond the scattered couples at picnic benches, looking for a treeless stretch of grass. He wondered if the picnickers were as in love as he felt.

Noticing a spot, he beckoned to Jemma and they

trotted onto the grassy expanse. Jemma took off running backward, creating a distance, and Philip stood still, facing her. She looked like a young girl, sheathed in faded jeans and a pale pink T-shirt. She motioned she was ready, and Philip curled his wrist and let the plastic disk fly through the air.

Jemma leaped and caught it, flinging it back in one smooth motion. He caught the disk and made a good return. Tossing it back and forth like pros, they ran and jumped to make perfect catches. Philip rallied, realizing he was doing pretty well for a man of fifty.

Out of nowhere, a dog's ferocious bark distracted him. Wary, he glanced over his shoulder and saw a large chocolate Lab darting toward him, followed by a man in pursuit. His back was to Jemma, so the Frisbee sailed past. He flinched, sorry he'd missed, but praying the dog wasn't as vicious as his bark.

"Sorry," the fellow called, nabbing the dog's collar and bending down to capture the plastic disk. He kept his distance. "He's usually gentle, but he saw a squirrel." He shrugged apologetically, then lifted the Frisbee. "Should I toss it to you or pitch it back to your daughter?"

Philip's stomach tumbled, and he swiveled his head, praying Jemma hadn't heard. She stood too far back and her smile let him know she hadn't. Philip forced a pleasant expression and extended his arm. "Toss it here. Thanks."

"I'll keep this mutt out of your way," the man

said, clasping the dog's collar and guiding him back to the table.

Philip stared at the disk, then at the young man—he guessed him to be, at the most, twenty—and wondered if the rest of the world thought he was Jemma's father.

"What's wrong?" Jemma called.

Hearing her voice, he turned and beckoned to her. He'd lost his spirit for the game and was struggling to maintain his composure.

She scurried to him. "The dog didn't bite you, did he?"

Philip gave a lighthearted chuckle. "No, just distracted me." He glanced around at the young man. "I thought we ought to get going. I'm getting hungry, aren't you?"

"Now that you mention it, yes." She wrapped her arm around his and headed across the grass.

He wanted to uncouple his arm from hers, fearing the fellow was watching and wondering why a "father and daughter" looked so cozy. Shame rustled through Philip's mind. If Jemma wasn't ashamed, why should he be?

Instead of finding an excuse to free himself, he squeezed her hand and sent up a prayer that God would teach him to be concerned about things of importance and enjoy the love that Jemma offered so openly.

Jemma looked out the window, waiting for Philip. Tonight was the Chamber of Commerce icebreaker, and her nerve endings knotted with anxiety. For the past couple of days, Philip had been trying to hide something, but Jemma sensed something was wrong.

Their day at the park had been wonderful, but when they stopped to eat, Philip became withdrawn, as if his thoughts were miles away. She'd asked, but as always he denied that he was troubled. He'd wasted his time trying to soothe her with denials. Jemma had gotten to know him better than he knew himself. He wasn't fooling her at all, and she planned to get to the bottom of his distress. She prayed it wasn't something she had done.

Jemma glanced down at her outfit, tan slacks and jacket with a black silk tunic. It would do. Casual yet dressy. She hoped Philip approved. As always, a few wispy curls had escaped as she pulled back her hair with a black scrunchee.

Hearing Philip's car pull into the driveway, she grabbed her shoulder bag and headed down the stairs, eager to begin the evening.

When she opened the front door, Philip met her on the porch. He stepped back, a pleased look brightening his face. "You look great." He touched her shoulder and ran his finger along the collar of her jacket, then caught an unruly curl and tucked it behind her ear.

She stepped back, brushing her hands down the jacket to the trousers. "Are you sure this is okay? I didn't know how casual was casual…if you know what I mean.''

His sweet smile sent her pulse jumping.

"Perfect. Casual, but elegant. You always look good to me," he said.

"You don't look too bad yourself." He looked perfect to her in his navy-blue slacks and a mock turtleneck under his carmel-colored sport coat.

"Thanks. I accept all compliments." His warm smile burrowed through her chest while he slid his arm around her waist and guided her to the car.

As they drove across town, Jemma longed to ask him about his problem—what was it that troubled him, but the time didn't seem right. Instead, she talked about Claire's latest antics and the wonderful comments she'd received from guests since launching the morning baskets.

He listened and offered brief comments, but she knew he was distracted. Tonight would be stressful for Philip. The party was her debut on his arm. She was his date. His younger woman.

She wanted to say she didn't care what people thought, but she did. Anything that wounded Philip tore at her, too. When his face flinched with concern and his tender eyes filled with hurt, the same emotions surged through Jemma, as if they were connected by a thin cord of shared emotions. She'd seen her own fear and despair in Philip's eyes too often not to acknowledge the phenomenon.

In the parking lot, Philip turned off the motor, and

Jemma stepped from the car with her most charming smile, prepared for the worst. Leers and snide comments she hoped she could handle. *Sticks and stones can break my bones*—the childhood rhyme bounced through her mind. But could she handle Philip's stress tonight?

When he opened the hall door and she stepped inside, determination pushed Jemma forward. With a smile plastered on her face, she captured Philip's arm and marched into the room.

Philip paused for a moment, then gave a wave and moved forward, nodding to individuals as he passed. "Don," Philip said, extended his hand, "it's good to see you."

"It's been too long," the man said, his eyes focused on Jemma. "And who is this lovely young lady?"

"This is my friend, Jemma Dupre."

"Don Bratten," he said, shaking Jemma's hand. "It's nice you could come. You have a new business in town?"

His question ruffled Jemma. "No, Philip and I are friends."

"Ooh." He flashed Philip a devious smile. "My wife couldn't make it. She's the president of the PTA." He shrugged. "Their meeting is tonight."

"You have children, then," Jemma said, trying to think of something to shift the conversation.

"Two kids. Son and daughter. Elementary school. And you?" Don asked.

"None." She wanted to say *none yet,* but the comment was too presumptuous and far too intimate.

"Someday, I hope," he said, his gaze shifting from Jemma to Philip. He grabbed Philip's arm, giving it a good-old-boy shake. "You look great, Philip. What have you been up to?" He shifted his focus again to Jemma and back to Philip.

Jemma wanted to crawl away. Had she heard an innuendo in his tone, or was it her imagination? She moved back a couple of steps and braced herself against an empty chair.

Philip glanced her way before answering Don. "Listen, I need to take care of the lady here. We'll talk later." He gripped the man's shoulder and turned to Jemma.

"Let's get a drink, and I'll introduce you to some of the others."

Jemma followed, but wanted to run out the door and save him the emotional trauma of introductions. No matter how she took Don's comments and looks, she felt on display. And she was sure Philip felt more miserable than she.

At the bar, she asked for a tonic with lime, and took a sip while Philip ordered his drink. When they walked away, she caught his sleeve. "Listen, I could say I'm ill and we can leave. I don't want to put you through this."

Philip saw the reeling emotions on her face—panic, hurt, confusion—and his frustration rose. He had been as guilty as Don. Why hadn't he said,

"This is my lady friend?" *My lady.* She was his lady not his "lady friend," and he wasn't going to let a stranger in the park or an associate with his mind in the sewer ruin a relationship that he'd nearly destroyed himself.

Her concerned expression powered his resolve. "Absolutely not. I've looked forward to this day."

Though he'd exaggerated, at the moment Philip meant every word. He slipped his arm around her waist and guided her across the room to a small cluster of businesspeople he'd known for years.

This time he did it right. "This is my lady, Jemma Dupre," he said to the group in general, and then introduced Jemma one by one.

Maybe their looks of acceptance were only wishful thinking on his part, but he didn't believe so. Each seemed gracious. When he introduced Jemma to the owner of the town bookstore, Gracie Dobson extended her hand with a lovely smile.

"Jemma, how nice to meet you. I've wondered why this handsome man never had a beautiful woman on his arm. Today I can stop asking." She leaned over and gave Jemma a hug.

A sweet flush bathed Jemma's creamy complexion, and her smile seemed as natural as a spring rain.

The rest of the evening passed with laughs and welcomes to the guests, and no one said a word, until Don cornered Philip again when he was alone getting a soft drink.

"You old so-and-so," Don said, a leering grin on

his face. "Where'd you pick up that young chick?" Don squeezed his upper arm again with an irritating shake. "You enjoying the young stuff?"

Slowly, Philip shifted his eyes from the man's grip to his face. "I didn't pick her up, Don. God sent her to me. She's terrific."

"I'll bet she is."

Tension shot up Philip's back and he knotted his fist.

Don dropped his hand and closed his gaping mouth. "Listen, buddy, I didn't mean to offend—"

"And *enjoying* isn't the word," Philip said. "I cherish her, and I'd like her to be my wife...only I haven't asked her yet."

"Hey, man," Don said, his face sheet white, "I'm sorry, and I wish you both the best. She's beautiful, and I was a slob to say anything."

"You were, Don, but I have to forgive a man who recognizes a beautiful woman when he sees one." He turned away, not wanting to waste his breath to explain that Jemma was even more lovely on the inside.

Heading back to Jemma, Philip's pulse surged as he realized what he had said. *I'd like her to be my wife.* Tonight was the first time he'd allowed his heart to speak what he'd felt for so long. His mind whirred with thoughts. He'd propose, but when? What was the right place and time? And Claire. He should talk with Claire. He had many questions and concerns to sort out. She was Jemma's closest family, and it seemed only right.

He headed back to Jemma feeling on top of the world.

Chapter Fourteen

A warm sunny breeze turned the September afternoon into an Indian summer evening. Philip entered the boutique from the front, hoping that Claire was ready to close the shop. He wanted to talk in private, uninterrupted by customers.

When he opened the door, the bell's tinkle brought Claire in from the back room. "Philip, it's you. Good. I was afraid it was a customer. I'm getting ready to close."

"Then, I timed it right." He gave her a hug. "Do you have time to talk?"

"Sure. What's up?" She looked into his eyes, then clutched the doorjamb. Her face filled with worry. "It's not Andrew, is it? Did something happen—?"

"No, it's not Andrew. I haven't heard from him since my birthday dinner. I just want to talk."

"Whew, you scared me." She arched a penciled

brow and grinned. "I hope I haven't missed a loan payment."

He wrapped his arm around her shoulder. "We're not talking about you. It's about me...and Jemma."

She spun around, her hands clasped near her chest and an eager smile on her lips. "You and Jemma? Well, praise the Lord. Maybe he does listen to this old gal."

He didn't comment. Instead, he walked to the front door, turned the lock and flipped over the Closed sign.

Claire gave the shop a once-over, and when he reached her by the side door, she snapped off the light and he followed her up the stairs.

"So what's this about?" she asked, huffing as she climbed the steps, peeking occasionally over her shoulder as if he were a fish she feared might escape.

"From that grin on your face, you know what it's about," Philip said, springing up the steps behind her and feeling younger than he had in years.

At the top, she swung around. "Does Jemma know you're here?"

He shook his head. "No. But she will soon."

Her look lifted his spirits. Though he had assumed Claire would be pleased, his old inner fear nagged at him, and once in a while his confidence flagged. Sometimes Philip wondered if God was really guiding his path or if it was his desire.

"Sit," Claire said as they entered the kitchen. "How about some coffee?"

"Sounds good, but nothing to eat. I'm taking Jemma out to dinner."

Filling the coffeemaker, Claire fluttered at the counter, her arms and mouth racing like thoroughbreds in a derby.

"This has been my dream, Philip." She flashed him a smile. "I tried to drop hints to Jemma that you'd make a good husband, but you know Jemma."

He did, and he nodded, but Claire rattled on.

"She had this need to be independent. I guess I can't blame her when I think back..."

Philip's mind drifted to the first day he had laid eyes on Jemma. She had been standing on the ladder, her face turned away, but from behind he had seen her delicate figure and her quaking knees.

He'd climbed up behind Jenna and grabbed her waist, and his heart had turned to jelly when she spun around. He'd tried not to laugh at the determination in her eyes as she pushed him away with one hand while clinging to the rung with the other.

"What's so funny?" Claire asked.

Philip jumped at her question. "Jemma. Your description tickled me."

"Oh," she said, "I thought you weren't listening."

He knew he'd better tune in before she gave him a quiz.

Claire rested her elbows on the table and folded her hands together as if in prayer. "So now...tell me about you and Jemma."

He realized she'd slid a cup of black coffee in front of him and another with milk for herself. Philip picked up the mug and took a sip.

"First, I came for your blessing, Claire, but...to be honest it's more than that." He stared at the cup, afraid to see the look in her eyes. "No matter how you cut it, I'm old enough to be Jemma's father."

"Philip, don't be ridiculous. There's age, and then there's age. You're young at heart. You're a hand-some, virile, generous man, whether you think it or not. Did you ever take look at yourself? If not, you should. You might be pleasantly surprised."

Her comment had a ring of familiarity. Ian had said something similar. But he needed more than a compliment. When he focused on Claire's face, he recognized sincerity. She wasn't just trying to make him feel better. He lowered his head.

"I suppose I ought to take a gander."

When he lifted his eyes, her face had darkened, and she gripped his forearm. "Philip...you're not telling me...that you have, uh, problems, are you? I mean are you worried that you...can't—"

Philip loosed a loud, shocked guffaw. "Oh, Claire, no." Heat flew to his face. Why would she think such a thing?

"I'm sorry, but you've moped about old age since I came to Loving. I thought maybe that's what was worrying you." She swept her hands toward the ceiling. "How was I to know?"

Nervous laughter punctuated his sentence. "When

you come right down to it, Claire, you shouldn't know...but I'm telling you that all of me functions well. I'm only fifty."

"Ah-ha," she exclaimed, "I'm glad you finally realize that."

Philip gaped at her, letting her words sink in. "You got me, Claire. I had no idea where you were leading me."

"I'm leading you home, Philip. Home to a young woman's arms."

Her face glowed like an angel's. She might be an exotic angel, but she was one just the same. "I'm hoping she'll accept me. I'd be lost if she—"

Claire's face filled with understanding. "She's nearly as dumb as you are, but I think when you ask the question you'll hear the answer you want." She lifted her cup and took a lengthy sip of coffee, watching him over the rim of the cup. "I think her fear was your faith. Never your age. And now she knows you're a Christian."

Philip nodded. "I hope she does."

"She does. Lyle Junior was a con-artist...like his father, I'm sorry to say. Jemma and I were both duped, but we stuck with them, hoping for change, hoping for some intangible fluke to make things right. We ladies don't give up easy."

Philip prayed Claire was correct. How could he go on if Jemma gave up on him?

"Jemma's as stubborn as a mule, but she's also

very faithful," Claire said. "And you can't say that about all women."

"Or men." His memory drifted back to men he knew who had cheated on their wives. He'd cheated on his wife, but with his work and ambition, not with another woman.

"So what else bothers you? I see it on your face."

Philip moved the mug around on the table, his mind organizing his thoughts, trying to put his finger on the fears that had come so close to harnessing his feelings for Jemma.

Finally he opened his mouth and revealed his list of fears—being a good husband, showing Jemma the love and attention she deserved, fathering children that he would be able to see grow into adults.

When he finished, Claire didn't respond. She rose and left the room, leaving Philip to stare after her, concerned and speechless.

In a heartbeat, she came through the doorway with a Bible in her hand. "I never read this much until recently," she said, "but since it's fresh in my mind, I'd like to read you something."

Philip blew out a slow stream of breath and leaned back against the chair, chiding himself for the thought that Claire had turned her back on him.

"This doesn't answer every question, but it does a pretty good job." She flipped through the crisp pages until she jammed her finger against one. "Right here in First Corinthians—the most beautiful words I've ever read. 'Love is patient, love is kind.

It does not envy, it does not boast, it is not proud. It is not rude, it is not self-seeking, it is not easily angered, it keeps no record of wrongs.' "

She paused and gave him a long knowing look before she continued. " 'It always protects, always trusts, always hopes, always perseveres. Love never fails. When perfection comes, the imperfect disappears. When I was a child, I talked like a child, I thought like a child, I reasoned like a child. When I became a man, I put childish ways behind me.' "

Philip gasped and dragged in a deep breath.

"Ever hear that before?" Claire asked.

"At weddings, I suppose."

"Couples should read this every night before going to bed and before going to work in the morning. Love has nothing to do with age or fears. It has to do with actions," she pressed her palm against her chest, "and what's in your heart."

His thoughts drifted over the words. *Patient, kind, protects, trusts.* He'd tried to show all those things to Jemma and more. He pictured their laughter, their love of nature, their tender looks and gentle touches.

"And here's the crux, Philip. 'When perfection comes, the imperfect disappears.' "

Claire had nailed it. When Jemma came into his life, God had given him another chance at perfection. Though his humanness had clung to his flaws and faults, he didn't have to face those anymore. Not with Jemma…and not with God.

He took Claire's hand. "Thank you. This talk is

worth a million dollars to me. That loan of yours is paid in full."

Her eyes widened and her head shook like a weather vane in a gale. "No, Philip, I wouldn't think of it."

"Yes, Claire, and I won't hear another word. I'll tear up your checks if you send them. Trust me."

She lifted her eyes. "Okay...but then let me add another two cents' worth...about the children."

Philip chuckled. "Two cents? I suppose you want change?"

She shooed away his comment. "Your father was eighty when he died. Now, if that's any sign, you'll have plenty of time to watch those little ones grow into adulthood." A deep laugh rumbled from her chest. "In fact, about the time they're teenagers, you'll probably wish God hadn't granted you quite so many years."

Philip smiled. He'd heard that sentiment many times, but wouldn't it be wonderful if the Lord gave him the opportunity to experience it himself.

Jemma skidded to a stop, and a high-pitched titter rose behind her. She stopped and looked over her shoulder. "What's so funny, Latrice?"

"Where are you going, girl?"

"I'm plodding today, Latrice. I'll never get finished. Judy is out, so I have to prep the baskets before I leave."

The woman slapped her leg. "Come on, now. You don't think the boss'll fire you?"

Jemma grinned. "Not fire me, but—"

"That man has eyes for you, girlfriend. Although I'm sure that's no surprise to you."

"Not anymore...but it took me a while to catch on."

She wrapped her arm around Jemma's shoulder. "I knew it the day he invented that job for you. He had love in his eyes."

Jemma froze to the spot. Reining in her shock, she monitored her voice. "What job?" She remembered thinking that he'd hired too many housekeepers. She'd told Philip that.

"Come on, girl...the one you're in now."

Icy tendrils gripped her heart. "You mean..." Her voice shook and she swallowed her panic. "Specialty Director."

Latrice nodded, her grin as wide as a rainbow. "We never had a position like that around here until you came along."

Jemma willed a lighthearted smile to her face, wanting to die.

"I remember when Carrie came gigglin' to me about that job. She and I had a good laugh. We figured he'd confess...or you'd just hear it through the grapevine."

"That old grapevine," Jemma sang out, her heart hammering until she thought her chest would explode. She gripped the cart handle for support.

"Well, I need to get moving. Even if I'm in cahoots with the boss, I don't want to spend the night here."

Latrice clasped her shoulder. "No, girl, you have better things to do with your time. You get along."

She sent Jemma a cheerful wave and hurried around the corner, leaving Jemma clinging to the cart with trembling hands and wondering what to do.

Anger sizzled inside her. She wanted to tear into Philip's office and toss a morning basket in his face. The grapevine would get a kick out of that! Even the thought tore at her, knifed her with pain. How could Philip have set her up to look like such a fool? Why did he think no one would ever tell her that she'd been another of his charity cases?

She'd gone on his research trips, raced around the hotel like she had a purpose, and all the while the staff was laughing behind her back.

And Philip? Even if that's how it had started, why hadn't he told her? She cringed, knowing the answer. If he had admitted it, she would have ripped and snorted like a wild bull. Tears welled in her eyes. But…they would have made up, and maybe laughed about it later.

But not now.

Avoiding Latrice, Jemma headed back to her workroom and called Ian. "I'm not feeling well, Ian. Can you replace me for the rest of the day? I really need to go home."

Ian sent her on her way, and Jemma slipped out of the building. When she reached the outside, tears streamed down her face while she hurried to her car, praying no one would see her. She had to get home.

Inside the car, she closed her eyes. *Dear Lord, why? Why did he hurt me so badly? Philip isn't like Lyle, so why did he deceive me? Please help me.*

Her hopes and dreams slipped away like sand beneath her feet—like the beautiful evening when they'd wandering along the shore in her stockinged feet. Washed away.

Philip sat with his face buried in his hands. What had happened and where had she gone? He'd called her apartment, he'd called Claire. He didn't understand.

Ian had said she came to him midway through the day, saying she was sick and needed to go home. But she wasn't there. Claire knew nothing. His only option was to go to Jemma's apartment. But why didn't she answer the telephone? A horrible fear filled his mind. No. He had to be wrong.

His hand clung to the telephone, his head pounding. Philip rose and, after making an excuse to his secretary, rushed from the building.

His mind flew as fast as he was driving, and when he pulled in front of her apartment, Jemma's car was there. He tried to calm himself. Maybe she'd only been sleeping when he called.

He hurried to the porch, opened the front door and climbed the stairs. Outside her door, he faltered, trying to calm himself. He was being foolish.

Philip tapped and called her name. He listened. Nothing. She had to be there. Her car was outside. This time he knocked louder and tried the doorknob. It was locked.

Mrs. Luddy. He glanced down the stairs, wondering if she was home and if she might know something. With another unanswered knock, he hurried down the stairs and tapped on the landlady's door. From inside, he heard footsteps and he waited.

"May I help you?" she said, peeking through the cranny of the half-opened door. "Oh, it's you." She swung the door open.

"I hate to bother you, but Jemma came home sick today and…she's not answering the telephone or her door. I'm afraid—"

Her face paled. "Let me get my key," she said, darting away from the door.

She returned in a moment, and he followed her up the stairs, fear gripping his heart. The woman gave a loud rap and waited. When Jemma didn't answer, she shot Philip a fearful look and pushed the key into the lock.

Philip held his breath while she inched open the door and called again.

This time, he heard Jemma's distant voice.

"You all right?" the landlady asked. "Can I come in?"

"Are you alone?" Her voice sounded weak.

Philip felt a shiver of fear. He couldn't imagine

why she would ask that question. He grabbed the door and pushed it open.

"Please," the woman said, cautioning him with her scowl. "It's me...and Mr. Somerville. Can we come in?"

"No." Jemma's voice grew louder. "I don't feel like seeing anyone now."

"Jemma, please," Philip called. "Let me in."

"No. Just go. I'll feel better tomorrow. I don't want anyone seeing me like this."

Jeanette shot him a "don't you dare step one foot inside this apartment" look, and he released his hold on the door and stepped back.

"Are you sure you're okay?" he asked.

"Yes."

Jeanette shrugged and closed the door. She slipped in the key and turned the lock, then dropped the key in her pocket. "I'll check on her later. We'd better do as she asks."

Philip shook his head. "I've never seen her act like this. I don't understand."

"You never know about women, Mr. Somerville. We have our good and bad days, you know. Be patient."

Be patient. How could he?

Mrs. Luddy grasped his arm and turned him toward the stairs. "She asked to be alone. And that's what we're going to do. Leave her be."

"May I call you later?" Philip asked, his head pounding unmercifully.

"Sure, I'll give you my number."

He followed her down the stairs, wrapped in confusion and frustration. Waiting outside her door for the number, Philip looked up the staircase and longed to dash to the top, throw his weight against the door and break in to see what was wrong.

He heard the landlady's steps and turned back to her.

"Here you go," she said, handing him a slip of paper. "Wait a couple of hours. I'll check on her later."

He stared at the paper. "Thank you," he said before grabbing the doorknob and bolting from the house. Jemma had never been moody. Something was wrong. Something that he had or hadn't done. Something...

But what could it be?

Chapter Fifteen

❧

"Thanks, Jeanette," Jemma said.

"Don't you worry. I'll tell him what you told me."

Jemma closed the door as the landlady's steps faded on the stairs. She felt terrible about putting poor Jeanette in the middle of the situation. She'd used a headache as the excuse for her earlier behavior, but it had been difficult to explain why to keep Philip away.

She needed time to think...although she'd done some serious thinking already. After Jeanette and Philip had left earlier in the day, Jemma had telephoned Bay Breeze. She couldn't talk with Philip, and Ian wasn't at his desk, so she left her resignation on voice mail. Her absence would cause difficulty for her co-workers, and she regretted that. It wasn't them, but Philip who had hurt her so deeply.

After she'd left the message, she thought about what she would do now. Leave town? Work for another resort? Now that she'd gained confidence, she could do anything. Her chin rose with pride, then dropped with reality.

Philip. She loved him. She'd trusted him. How could he have neglected to tell her the truth about the position...especially after he'd said he loved her? Or had that been a lie, too?

Where would she go now? Philip would probably show up again and she didn't want to see him—yet she needed to talk. She eyed the telephone. Claire. If anyone understood and cared, it was Claire.

She punched in the familiar numbers and waited. When she heard Claire's voice, her throat constricted and she swallowed hard before she could speak.

"What's wrong?" Claire's voice rose with concern.

"Not on the telephone. Can I come there?"

"You don't have to ask, Jemma. Are you sure you're okay?"

"Yes, I just need to talk." Jemma's voice trembled with emotion.

"Then, I'll be waiting."

She hung up, grabbed her handbag and darted down the stairs. With a quick comment to Jeanette, she drove away from the house, looking behind her for Philip's car.

Jemma realized she might be acting foolishly, but she felt forsaken. Like a nightmare, Latrice's comments had dragged her into a whirlpool of humiliation, and no matter how hard Jemma tried, she couldn't wake up. The deception had been real.

She parked on the side street and walked through the alley to the boutique. When she closed the side door, Claire stood on the landing, waiting for her. Before Jemma reached her mother-in-law, a torrent of tears rolled down her cheeks.

"What is it?" Claire's generous arms embraced her, clasped Jemma's cheek against her bosom and patted her head as if Claire were a mother consoling her child.

"I'm sorry, Claire." She wiped the tears from her eyes and went ahead of her mother-in-law into the apartment.

"I made some tea," Claire said. "Go sit in the living room, and I'll bring in the pot."

She did as her mother-in-law said and dropped into the familiar sofa, hearing the *clank* and *ting* of Claire's movements in the kitchen.

Jemma's body ached almost as much as her heart did. She sorted through her thoughts, trying to decide where to begin.

Hearing a rustle, Jemma looked up as Claire swept into the room with the tea tray. Claire slipped it on the table, poured a mug for Jemma and sank into a chair with her own.

"Now, tell me what's wrong," Claire said.

With the details spinning in her head, Jemma told

the story from beginning to end. Latrice's news, Philip's frantic visit and Jeanette's kind assistance.

"So I called Bay Breeze and left Ian a voice mail that I was leaving—that I wouldn't be back." Her voice caught.

"I can't believe you did that, Jemma. Time is a healer. I can understand that you're upset. Philip was wrong not to tell you. But you haven't heard his side of the story. You—"

"What side could there be, Claire?" Digging into every corner of her reasoning, Jemma could see no excuse for Philip's behavior. "I trusted him. I opened my heart to him...and I was being laughed at by my co-workers."

"Laughed at? Why do you say that?"

"Latrice said—"

"You told me Latrice said that she and that other woman—"

"Carrie," Jemma said.

"Yes. Carrie and Latrice had *giggled*. Giggling and laughing at someone aren't the same. And what had they found funny? Was it your position, or realizing that Philip had eyes for you?"

Claire's words knocked the wind out of Jemma's anger. *Pride*. She'd allowed it to overcome her wisdom. Jemma thought through the situation again, trying to remember exactly what Latrice had said.

"Am I right?" Claire's voice was gentle.

Brushing the tears from her chin, Jemma could

only nod. "But it's too late. I resigned, and I'm not calling back to say I changed my mind."

Claire rose and lifted the teapot. "Now, I want you to stop talking and second-guessing. Thinking got you into this mess." She tilted the spout and filled Jemma's cup, then replaced the pot and sank back into the chair.

"Listen to me, Jemma. It's never too late."

Philip pressed his ear against the receiver, listened to the unanswered ring and dropped the telephone onto the cradle. Last night, he'd done what Jemma had asked. He'd called the landlady that evening, and she had said that Jemma would talk to him tomorrow. Tomorrow was here. But where was she?

He drummed his fingernails against the mahogany desk and stared through the window at the whitecaps rolling in to shore. No guests stood on the pier or lolled on the sand. Only a few hungry seagulls hopped along the deserted beach, looking through the washed-up shells and driftwood for a scrap of food.

"Philip."

Hearing Ian's voice coming out of nowhere, Philip jumped. He swung around at breakneck speed.

"Sorry," Ian said.

Looking at his assistant's face, Philip knew something was terribly wrong. "What is it?"

"It's Jemma."

Philip's heart kicked into passing gear. "What's wrong with her?"

Ian shook his head. "She resigned."

"Resigned?" Philip's mind reeled with confusion.

Ian stepped closer to the desk. "She's leaving Bay Breeze. She left a message on my voice mail last night. What happened? Why did she resign?"

Philip lifted his eyes to Ian's bewildered face. "Resigned? I can't believe it."

"You didn't know?"

"She was upset—but resign? Why would she do that?"

Ian sat across from him. "When she called, she sounded terrible. Her voice was trembling, and she said she needed to go home. She was sick." He paused. "I believed her, Philip."

Philip swiveled in the chair and looked out the window, feeling as desolate as the shore. "I'm not blaming you, Ian." Who had talked with Jemma yesterday? Who would know something? Carrie? Latrice?

"Would you ask Latrice if she talked with Jemma? Maybe she knows something." He rubbed his eyes. "Maybe she's in the hospital."

"Who? Latrice?" Ian asked.

Philip shook his head. "No, Jemma. If she's not home now, maybe she's in the hospital or seeing her doctor."

Ian rose. "I'll find Latrice for you." He stood up, then darted for the door.

Philip stared at the telephone. He hated to bother the landlady, but worry motivated him to pull the number from his wallet and pick up the receiver. He called, listened. No answer.

Fear sent his heartbeat on a gallop. He pushed the button and punched in Claire's number. He let it ring, knowing she might be with a customer.

"Loving Treasures." Claire's deep voice flowed through the line.

"Have you seen Jemma today, Claire?"

"No...I haven't, Philip," she said.

But he sensed something in her tone. "Did you talk with her? I'm in a panic here, Claire. Where is she?"

"I don't know, Philip. I thought she was home."

"Did you talk with her...yesterday?"

He heard an intake of breath. "Yes, she was here."

"There? What do you mean?" Philip's mind grasped at the shred of information.

Silence lengthened on the line.

"Claire! What do you mean?"

"Philip. Calm down. Jemma's fine. She was here. We talked."

"Fine? She was ill." He hit his fist against the desk.

"Well...yes, she looked terrible. But I'm sure she's better today." She drew in another lengthy breath. "If not today, then tomorrow."

"You're not making sense, Claire. Tell me what's wrong...please."

"Look, Philip. I can't share what we discussed. It's between Jemma and..."

He waited. "And who? Me?"

"I've said enough. Be patient. She'll come around."

"Tell me what's wrong, Claire. I love her."

"You've gotten all you're getting from me. I know that's unusual, but it's the truth."

She covered the telephone and spoke to someone. "I have to go, Philip. I have customers."

Before he could say goodbye or thank you, she'd hung up, leaving him more confused than before.

He stared at the phone, wanting to call someone—someone who'd make sense out of it all. But no one came to mind.

The phone's ring sent his pulse charging through him. He nabbed the receiver.

"Claire?"

Silence.

Jemma. He closed his eyes. "Jemma?"

"Philip?"

Andrew. Philip's endurance was ebbing, and his problem-filled mind was too weary to deal with another situation, but he hadn't heard his brother's voice in months. "Andrew, how are you?"

"Is something wrong, Philip?" Andrew's quiet voice was filled with concern.

"No...yes, well, I have a few problems here, but I'm fine."

More silence.

"Is something wrong with you?" Philip asked. He prayed not—he couldn't handle another thing.

"I'm thinking of coming home…that is, if you'll have me."

Coming home? "What do you mean, if I'll have you?" He ached for his brother. "You want to come back to Bay Breeze?"

"Not as a partner. I know that's impossible. But if I come home I'll need a job…something until I can get started again."

A mixture of irritation and compassion shuffled through Philip. He stared down at the mouthpiece, not sure what to say.

"I'm not destitute," Andrew said. "I have a little money, but I don't want to jump into anything. I need to make some long-term plans…get my thoughts together." He cleared his throat. "The one thought that has come together is…I'd like to come home."

Philip's irritation melted. "You're always welcome here, Andrew. I'll find something for you—if you want it."

"Nothing big. Maintenance, if that's all you have."

His brother would never be a partner, but Philip could certainly give him work…a job he could hold with pride. "We'll talk when you get here."

"Thanks. You'll never know how good it feels to hear you say that."

"Andrew, when will you come?" Philip lifted his

eyes and saw Latrice standing in the doorway, her brown skin ashen.

"I'm not sure. A few months if that's okay. I have some things to settle first."

"Call me when you decide."

Andrew said goodbye before Philip had to end the conversation. Philip set the telephone in the cradle and beckoned to Latrice.

"I hear Jemma resigned," she said, her eyes wide and concerned.

"Did you talk with her yesterday?"

The housekeeper nodded. "In the hallway upstairs. But she was fine then. We were joking and laughing."

"Laughing?" He couldn't imagine Jemma being lighthearted, as sick as she had been. "What was so funny?"

"Well, I saw her barreling down the corridor like someone held a whip..."

Latrice told her story word for word, and Philip's chest ached with despair. The poor woman had no idea what she'd done.

"She did know, Mr. Somerville, didn't she? No one thought anything of it. No one."

A look of grief filled her dark eyes, and Philip shook his head. "No, I'd never had the courage to tell her, Latrice, but it's not your fault. It's mine. I should have."

"But what can I—"

"Nothing." He rose and came around the desk.

"You can do nothing, but I can. Go back to work and don't worry. I'm glad you told me what happened. Thank you."

The woman lowered her face into her upraised hands. "I'm so sorry, Mr. Somerville. So sorry."

He wrapped his arm around her shoulder with as much comfort as he could give and walked her to the doorway. When she'd gone, he closed the door and braced his back against the sturdy wood. He had no idea what to do. He needed to talk with Jemma.

But what would he say? He had no excuse. His feeble alibi sailed away like chaff. He closed his eyes and prayed that the Lord would give him the answer.

His chest ached and his lungs felt as if they would burst. He needed air. Opening the door, he walked past his secretary and into the corridor. He took a side exit and strode across the grass, around the building and down the path to the beach.

Looking behind him, he saw his balcony jutting from the building—the place where he'd first said "I love you" to Jemma. Sorrow squeezed his heart.

He turned away, unable to bear the pain, and scanned the horizon, watching the waves roll in churning with white foam. He'd have to put the boat in dry dock soon. His focus drifted to the sailboat, rocking in the surf—and he walked along the path and took the stairs down the hill to the boat dock. Standing on the pier, his gaze riveted to the large black letters. *My Lady.*

He'd been wrong thinking the boat would be the

last woman in his life. Jemma had pried open his starving spirit and nurtured it with her love. *She* was his lady...and the only one that would live in his heart.

Jemma steered her car toward the resort. She prayed that Philip would speak with her. She'd acted horribly—so unforgiving, as Claire had pointed out. How could she say that she was a Christian and be unwilling to forgive?

The problem had been her pride, her fear that people were laughing behind her back. An old insecurity. But her talk with Claire had put everything into perspective. Latrice hadn't said her co-workers had laughed at her. Only that she and Carrie had giggled about Philip so obviously falling in love—in love with her.

His generosity and goodness filled her mind. Philip had stepped into her life and made her feel like a woman. Made her feel whole and complete. Yet she'd run away without a word. Without giving him a chance to defend himself.

A defense that was unnecessary, since the problem had been hers. Pride.

Thanking God for returning her to reason, she'd listened to Claire and then faced the truth. Philip had done nothing but behave like himself. A humanitarian. A man filled with kindness and compassion. A man who cared so much about her that he chanced his own workers' scorn by giving her a good job.

She treasured him…loved him more than she loved herself.

The scenery blurred as she pulled into the resort parking lot. She turned off the engine and brushed the tears from her eyes. What would she do if Philip said he'd had his fill of her? Her bullheaded determination, her lack of patience, her pride.

Bowing her head, she lifted her fear to the Lord. Even if Philip turned her away, she would fall to her knees and ask his forgiveness and thank him for all he'd done. With his help, Jemma felt able to find a job and to live on her own—and to feel good about herself.

Except right now.

Sitting in the car, Jemma looked at the building, quiet today with fewer guests and cooler weather. She took a deep calming breath, then grabbed her shoulder bag and slipped from the car.

Lord, let him be in his office and alone. She couldn't bear to sit in the waiting room with former co-workers gawking at her and wondering why she'd come back. The thought humbled her. She deserved nothing more.

Drawing her shoulders back, she hurried inside the employee door and headed toward Philip's office. His secretary only shrugged when she glanced into his empty room. Disappointed, Jemma turned and followed the corridor, wondering which way to head. In the lobby, she stopped and looked out at the water—lonely and deserted. The way she had felt since she'd walked away.

"Jemma."

She turned and faced Ian. "Hello, Ian. Have you seen Philip?"

"A while ago...through the window. He looked like he was headed for the beach."

"The beach? Thanks." She turned toward the door.

"Jemma?"

She swung back and looked at him.

"I just want to say..." Obviously uncomfortable, he looked down at the floor. "Well...I think you're the best thing that ever happened to Philip." He lifted his eyes. "I just wanted you to know."

Her heart swelled at his comment. "Thank you," she said, moving forward and embracing him. "He's the best thing that ever happened to me." She spun around and hurried through the door.

Following the path, Jemma searched the pier and shoreline without success. And then she thought about the sailboat and turned her eyes toward *My Lady*.

Philip stood on the dock, his hands in his pocket, his head bent, looking as desolate as she felt. Hurrying across the sidewalk, she headed down the hill and when her shoes hit the boat dock, Philip turned around.

"Jemma," he cried, racing toward her.

She flew toward him, leaping into his arms, tears

flowing down her cheeks. "Forgive me. I've been stupid and stubborn—"

"And bullheaded and unapproachable...and I love every contrary inch of you. There's nothing to forgive. You're my lady. My woman. My wife...if you'll have me."

She pulled her cheek away from his tear-dampened shirt and gazed into his tender eyes. "I treasure you...always. You're my life. My love."

Slipping his finger beneath her chin, Philip lifted her face to his and brushed his lips against hers. "I love you."

His words tangled in eager lips and trembling sighs, and when they drew back, Philip nuzzled his cheek against her windblown hair and thanked God for opening his eyes and his lonely heart.

He turned Jemma to face the gray waves. Together they watched them dash to the shore, dragging debris and sand into the swirly foam. Yet over it all, the sun had sprinkled gold dust on the water, just as the Lord had wrapped Philip's life with Jemma's bright smile.

Philip encircled his arms around her slender frame. Love was wonderful.

Chapter Sixteen

Seven months later

Jemma gazed at herself in the full-length mirror, admiring the lovely gown that Claire had helped her select for the wedding. She swept her hand down the soft pink fabric. A few seed pearls and beads adorned the bodice; otherwise, the gown was simple but elegant. Maybe there was hope for Claire, after all.

When Philip's guest room door swung open, Jemma jolted. Claire darted into the room, her arm filled with flowers. "The florist got here finally. I've been waiting on pins and needles."

"Look how beautiful," Jemma said, burying her nose in the stephanotis, ivy and lily of the valley. The rich fragrance filled the air.

"And this—" Claire held up her tiara of pink flowers. "So much better than a veil."

Jemma faced Claire, who lowered the garland onto Jemma's hair and secured it with pins.

"What do you think?" Jemma asked.

"You look beautiful. And it's not just the gown and flowers, Jemma. It's you—your eyes, your smile. I've never seen you look more content and happy."

"Or more loved," Jemma added. She rose on tiptoes and kissed Claire's cheek. "Thank you for everything. For your love and—" Her voice caught in her throat and she couldn't speak.

"No tears today, my dear. Today's for smiles and celebration."

Jemma caught her arm. "Did Andrew make it? Is he here?"

Claire shook her head. "No, but he called and apologized. Something came up and he's been delayed. Philip will tell you. He'll come home eventually."

"Is Philip terribly disappointed?" A twinge of sadness settled in her chest for Philip and the brother-in-law she had yet to meet.

"How could he be disappointed today?" Claire brushed a wisp of curl away from her cheek. "The man's thrilled."

Claire headed for the door. "I'll be back in a minute. Take a deep breath, because it's just about that time."

Jemma did as she was told. She primped one more time in the mirror, catching the flash of the lovely diamond that Philip had given her the same day she'd run to him seven months earlier, ready to fall on her knees. He'd had it weeks earlier and had planned to propose on the sailboat.

Instead, they'd proclaimed their love on the windy boat dock where she'd had no need to beg for forgiveness. Philip had overlooked her behavior and understood. And he'd apologized for his own actions. Yet, Jemma loved her work and, in her heart, was pleased that he'd entrusted her with the responsibility of being his new Specialties Director.

That same evening they'd sat in Philip's rooms talking until the wee hours of the morning about their future—children, hopes and dreams. With her head on Philip's shoulder, Jemma had felt rich with God's blessing.

When they planned the wedding, Philip had expected to have the ceremony at the church, but Jemma had other thoughts. The first time he told her he loved her had been on the spacious penthouse balcony. He gave little argument when she suggested they be married there.

She and Philip had arranged it all. They'd replaced the wrought-iron furniture with chairs facing the French doors so that they could look at their guests and the lake they both loved.

"Ready?" Claire said, swinging through the door. "Everyone's seated."

Jemma closed her eyes, calming her heart and thanking the Lord for the gift—her second chance at living and loving.

Claire held the door, and Jemma stepped into the hall. She could see Philip waiting for her, and she longed to run and throw herself in his arms, but she reined her joy and walked regally like the bride she was.

He looked so handsome in his dark suit and white shirt with a silk tie. In his buttonhole, he wore a sprig of stephanotis, and when he saw her, his face glowed as brightly as the sun shining through the French panes.

"Are you disappointed about Andrew?" she asked.

His smile answered her question. "I'm happy he called. When he does come home, I'll throw a party."

Jemma kissed his cheek.

Arm in arm, they walked forward, Claire ahead of them, and when they reached the doorway, the smiles of friends and co-workers warmed Jemma's heart. She looked beyond the guests to the sun-speckled lake, today calm and peaceful—so much like her heart.

A spring breeze rustled her gown and the scent of new growth hung on the air. Standing along the lake, trees were bursting with leaf buds and new blossoms sprouted everywhere—fitting on the day when just as she and Philip would begin their new life together.

Philip took her hand, his gray hair glinting in the light. She loved every silver strand, every crinkle at his eyes, the curve of his mouth. She feared her heart would shatter with her overwhelming joy.

"Dearly beloved, we are gathered here..." The words lifted and swelled, rising on the breeze.

"I take you, Jemma..." Philip's hand held hers, his love-filled eyes capturing hers as he spoke.

Then, above the beating of her heart, Jemma heard her voice speaking the words. "I give you this ring..."

And when the last prayer soared to heaven, Philip held her hand as the preacher announced, "Ladies and gentleman, may I present Mr. and Mrs. Somerville."

Smiling into her husband's eyes, Jemma felt Philip's lips brush hers as he whispered two words that wrapped around her heart.

"My lady."

* * * * *

*If you enjoyed LOVING TREASURES,
you'll love Gail Gaymer Martin's
exciting new story for
Silhouette Romance:*

LET'S PRETEND...

*Available July 2002
Don't miss it!*

Dear Reader,

Michigan is a beautiful state, and traveling along Lake Michigan I was inspired to use it as a setting for a novel series. Many years ago on a vacation, I visited the Musical Fountain in Grand Haven, and it stirred me to visit there again a couple of years ago. Grand Haven has always stood out in my mind as a lovely city, and I modeled the imaginary town of Loving after it.

When I began this story, I thought about the story of Ruth and Naomi—a young woman who left her old life behind and followed her mother-in-law to a new land and a new love. The story inspired me to write this story about a younger woman who finds love with an older man.

Whether you are younger or older, I hope you enjoy Jemma and Philip's story. I hope to share more stories with you set in Loving, Michigan.

Gail Gaymer Martin

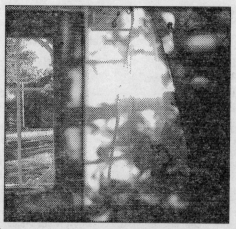